An Unusual Encounter

by

Howard S. Selden

A-Argus Enterprises International, Inc.
New Jersey***North Carolina

An Unusual Encounter © 2012
All rights reserved by
Howard S. Selden

A-Argus Better Book Publishers, LLC

For information:
A-Argus Better Book Publishers, LLC
9001 Ridge Hill Street
Kernersville, North Carolina 27285
www.a-argusbooks.com

ISBN: 978-0-6156380-4-1
ISBN: 0-6156380-4-X

Book Cover designed by Dubya

Printed in the United States of America

Dedication

To my children: David, Nathan and Rachel.

I like to think that my assorted stories were my most meaningful legacy. If it is true that authors inescapably insinuate themselves and give voice to their own prejudices and passions in their work, then so be it with mine. Thus a deeper understanding of their father might be gained. After all, the stories also belongs to them.

Also by Howard S. Selden

* * * * *The Pariah Stigma* * * * *
* * * * *The Shaman and the Jew* * * * *
* * * * *A Dental Odyssey [unlikely mus-
ings of a dentist]* * * * *
* * * * *Wapasha and the Rabbi* * * * *

Acknowledgments

The expanded format for this book was inspired by my article, *The Interview,* published in the online magazine, *The Jewish Magazine (www.jewishmag.com).*

Although many of the stories were invented, some were grounded in tales heard by the author, while others were based on real occurrences. Certain themes were also excerpted from my novels, *The Shaman and the Jew,* and *Wapasha and the Rabbi.*

Preface

Readers of my books—*The Shaman and the Jew* and *Wapasha and the Rabbi*—will likely recognize that this book qualifies as third in the series: the construct and subject matter were similar; with stories focused on dialogues between Jews and non-Jews, and their dynamic interrelationships. In addition, the fictionalized tales are all set within authentic historical frameworks.

To those first-time readers, let me extend a hearty welcome. I believe some insights into my concentration on particular subjects—along with a bit of my journey to authorship—will hopefully enrich your reading experience.

In my prior life as a dentist, I published many scientific articles of clinical interest, and following retirement found that I missed the writing, especially the solitary creativity.

Initially my efforts to find a suitable non-dental subject to write about proved more difficult than I imagined. For a while

I was frustrated and unsuccessful. When I eventually decided on fictional tales, based on, and inspired by events and issues that impacted and molded my life, I was energized. Why I was slow to recognize the obvious remains puzzling. But my progress was blocked by the emergence of unexpected concerns. I doubted whether I could write dispassionately enough about subjects which touched me emotionally, while sustaining the reader's interest. After all, although I didn't intend to write an autobiography, I still worried that too intense an involvement could adversely color and weaken the story telling. Yet, enthusiasm for the material was essential, and without it I knew I couldn't write. Absent such energy, my writing would stall. I was faced with an awkward paradox—on one hand eagerness and interest in the subject was essential; yet on the other hand too much emotional identification, with possible mawkish fervor, could undermine the balance and integrity of the writing.

Finally I arrived at what seemed a good compromise: I would indulge my imagination and tell a science fiction story.

To my satisfaction, the story flowed easily, and the rather provocative title, *The Pariah Stigma,* which came to mind before the writing began, was the key to the overriding theme. Though I believed the fictional format, with imaginative names, places and technologies, effectively disguised any connection to real life people and events, I was proved wrong. A friend quickly recognized the story for what it was—a metaphor for the history of the Jews. He was right. I had tried a fanciful approach, but its intent was more transparent than I imagined, and probably would be understood by many others. I was grateful for his insight; since it brought out into the open what I had hesitated to forthrightly deal with. The publishing of, *The Pariah Stigma,* served to restore my confidence—I was now ready to compose my stories, with measured dispassion. Without delay I embarked on a new book.

Before I go any further, I had better explain about the historic populations of European Jewery: they were divided into two broad groups—Ashkenazic and Sephardic. The need for this understanding will become clear.

The widely disseminated Jewish communities throughout most of central Europe, extending East, including Russia, were *Yiddish* ("the German/Hebrew colloquial language of the Jews") speakers, and came to be called Ashkenazic. Since all my ancestors were from this group, their many accomplishments, history, and inescapably including the Holocaust's ultimate catastrophe, were all part of my legacy.

The Sephardic group embraced Jews who lived historically in Spain and Portugal for many centuries, and whose descendants settled throughout the Middle East. Though both Jewish groups practiced essentially the same religion, the Sephardi never spoke *Yiddish*—they had evolved their own colloquial language known as *Ladino* ("a Spanish/Hebrew dialect").

My second book, *The Shaman and the Jew,* was essentially a Sephardic tale. On reflection, I now realize that my decision to write about this subject was not only influenced by the appeal of researching the history of a group I knew little about, with intriguing possibilities, but that I also had evaded the highly-charged story of my Ashkenazi heritage. In time, I faced that challenge.

In *The Shaman and the Jew,* the history of one Jewish/Persian family is traced through the generations, to their eventual settlement in Muslim controlled Spain, where they prospered for hundreds of years (hence, Sephardic derives from the Hebrew for Spain). The final overthrow of Muslim Spain by Christian armies in 1492 CE, also heralded the imposition of unrelenting persecution of Jews and Muslims, with suppression of their religions . . . by the infamous ecclesiastic 'Inquisition.' Moreover, Jews, as well as Muslims were no longer welcome in the country. In response to this horrific onslaught, the Jewish family, central to the story, surreptitiously sent their son to the New World. In a series of unforeseen events, he settled among a primitive, but welcoming tribe of Native Americans, where his Judaism flourished. Remarkably, his Old World religion successfully established a 'toehold' in America . . . long before the 1654 CE arrival in Dutch New Amsterdam (later conquered by the British and renamed New York) of a small group of Sephardic Jews—believed to be the first Jewish settlement in America.

Though I was launched as an author, with my spirits buoyed by my second published book, I still avoided the Ashkenazic tale. Instead I wrote a sort of hybrid Dental memoir entitled, *A Dental Odyssey: Unlikely Musings of a Dentist.*

Eventually, taking inspiration from the *Shaman and the Jew*, I expanded on the potential interaction of a Jew and non-Jew in the next book, *Wapasha and the Rabbi*—an Ashkenazic tale (finally waded in). The story's main characters are an old Polish Jew and a young Vietnam veteran, set within an unsettled contemporary America. Both seek a measure of tranquility and peace in a turbulent world. The war veteran suffers his own agonies with post-traumatic memories; and the elderly Rabbi, a survivor of the Holocaust, endures lingering anguish from his unforgettable emotional traumas. Unlikely as are these two dissimilar men—considerably divided in age, with an immense gulf of life's experiences—they nevertheless bonded. The vast differences were transcended as they recognized their common vulnerable humanity. Moreover, when they learned of each other's intimacy with cruelty and barbarism, a mutually fulfilling supportive relationship evolved.

I view all my stories, including those in this book—*An Unusual Encounter*—to exemplify that trials and tribulations are universal, experienced by people of all faiths and diverse backgrounds. No group has a monopoly on tragedy, or courage for that matter. What emerges for me, from individual acts of fortitude and struggles for survival, are how—despite the challenges—people can successfully restore enriched lives with purpose and meaning.

I am encouraged by the indomitable potential in all of us.

Howard S. Selden
Easton, Pennsylvania

Chapter One

Daryl Wincoat chose a clear, mild, sunny day when he expected Izak Asher would be out in the park, probably sitting on his usual bench. 'Sure enough,' mumbled Daryl to himself as he slowly walked along the black-topped park path, 'there he is, as if waiting for me. Now, I must remain cool, stroll over to him real easy, and act nonchalant. I don't want to alarm him.' Daryl nervously stroked his face for reassurance that he had actually shaved. He had long abandoned the daily ritual, and liked the overgrown stubble. Nervously he then checked the knot on his tie—his only tie, which he was unaccustomed to wear. He had made a special effort to appear respectable, not his usual unkempt, sloppy look. This interview was important, and he wanted to make a good impression.

While approaching Asher, his hand slipped down under his belt buckle as if to adjust his pants—but the move surreptitiously checked whether his fly was fully zipped. He was anxious about his fly, having already been embarrassed on several occasions when it was left open, to the delight of his bar cronies. Of course it only happened when he was seriously drinking—which he ruefully admitted had become too frequent. 'Well,' he said to himself, 'this interview will hopefully turn my luck around. I'll straighten everything out; and make a real start.'

Asher, deeply engrossed in reading his newspaper, was unaware of Daryl until he sat down at the other end of the bench. Asher turned, offered a friendly smile, and said,

"Welcome to my bench. For some reason people don't seem to enjoy the park much these days. I imagine a young fellow like yourself couldn't resist taking a breather from a hurried life, to spend some time out here among the trees, and maybe feed the squirrels and birds. They are so accustomed to folks that many will eat out of your hand. I think they recognize me. As soon as I sit down they gather around. I don't disappoint them. My bread crumbs are special. I lace them with some tasty bits from those Danish pastries available every morning at the Home, which the little creatures seem to relish. Personally, I don't like the Danish, and stick to my standard breakfast—a lightly toasted poppy seed bagel topped mit ("with") a generous schmear of grape jelly. Actually I alternate the grape with some delicious English orange marmalade, which I prefer to the overly sweet American concoctions. The English know how to cut the sweetness just enough with a tasty tartness. People accuse me of being in a rut, since I eat the same thing every morning. But I like it, and always look forward to breakfast. On the other hand, I observe that most folks use overly generous amounts of butter, not only on their bread but on hot cereals, and of course with vegetables at dinner. Years ago I lost my taste for butter, and now even find its appearance unappetizing. Did you ever notice how terribly oily melted butter looks? I'm not surprised they say butter's not good for you, and probably clogs your arteries. Of course my stomach shrunk-up many years ago when I somehow survived near starvation. I keep my trim figure easily because it takes so little to fill me up. To tell you the truth, the sight of too much food, especially when covered with a highly-seasoned gooey gravy makes me lose my appetite. I probably could live on bread alone . . . which I once did."

Daryl was taken aback by Asher's effusive, though friendly, conversation, which also roused a welcome wave of relief. *Wow,* he thought to himself, *what good luck that he broke the ice. I was in a sweat worrying how he would take to me. It looks like this interview will be a cinch.* Swallowing hard and forcing a smile he said,

"By the way, Mr. Asher, I'm Daryl Wincoat of the Herald newspaper. I hope you don't mind, but the folks at the Home directed me to you. You see, I've been told a big Jewish holiday is coming up soon, and my editor asked me to write a nice piece about it all. Actually, I'm at a disadvantage—I don't know anything about Jews and their religion. Now that I think about it, you might be the first Jew I ever spoke to. To be honest, religion is something I never could get a handle on, and that goes for all those Christian holy rollers. I was hoping you would sort of fill-me-in about this Jew stuff."

Daryl felt the moisture forming in his armpits, and his hands were real cold, as they always did when he was nervous. He wondered how Asher took his comments, and thought maybe he offended the old guy?

Asher had listened carefully, with his bright blue eyes focused on Daryl, and finally nodded slowly and asked with a permissive wave of his right hand,

"So, boychik, tell me, vos ("what") would you like to know?"

Daryl hesitated, not sure how to answer. He felt as if frozen, not able to think. His new journalist job was a welcome opportunity, but he worried that he might not have what it takes, and would fail. His first assignment couldn't have been worse—this Jewish thing was so foreign it disoriented his thinking; and he wasn't able to imagine an approach to the story, let alone ask meaningful questions.

Finally, Asher nodded again, as though coming to a thoughtful assessment, and with a determined look, said,

"First of all, let me tell you that I like your name. Daryl! It has a nice sound. It is so typically goyish, and American. Names are important, you know. I was told to change mine from Izak to Irving when I first came to this country. But, it sounded so strange I wouldn't have known myself. Izak has a lot of accumulated baggage, which a name change wouldn't wipe out. So, Izak I was, and always will be."

Daryl hurriedly fumbled to remove a small blank notebook and ballpoint pen—recently purchased—from the inside pocket of his careworn jacket. He was getting ready to take notes like a journalist, but so far he couldn't think of anything to write. His look of confusion and frustration was apparent, and an awkward silence followed.

Asher waited patiently. He had already warmed to the encounter, and was stimulated by the prospects of conversation with this stranger. He thought Daryl seemed a pleasant young man, though a bit unsettled, and clearly a novice journalist. *Well,* Asher philosophically concluded to himself, *everyone has to start someplace.* But he also noted Daryl's troubling eyes—he sadly recognized deep-seated pain and anguish. It was a look Asher was only too familiar with, which evoked his own unpleasant memories. Finally, mastering his emotions and managing a broad smile, he considered the potential in this unexpected encounter, and decided to encourage the dialogue. He put the newspaper down, turned sideways to look more directly at Daryl, and said,

"Daryl, if we're going to talk about the Jewish holidays we might have some problems. First of all, you should know there are more holidays than you can imagine, which incidentally in my opinion includes many that we really don't need. Actually, I warn you, dipping into Jewish lore is very challenging, to say the least. It is like entering a complex labyrinth, mit countless byways in which one can easily get lost. For our purposes, it probably would be helpful for you to start off learning a few simple Yiddish words. It'll get you into the mood and give you a feel for the subject. Yiddish is so natural to me the words just slip out. I often wonder whether I could express myself only in English?"

Daryl's blank expression and wrinkled brow readily revealed his tension and uncertainty. Finally he quietly stated ,

"You better start with that word, Yiddish. What does it mean? I never heard it before."

"Ah, a good place to begin," Asher replied. "Yiddish is really the invented language of the European Jews. Can you imagine that—a whole new language? Think of it as their lingua franca. Oops! There I go again with a foreign term, only this time I think it's Latin, or maybe Italian. It simply means the common spoken language. The Yiddish story gets much more complex. Should I go on?"

"Please do. I don't know anything about it, and I'm really interested," said Daryl, trying to sound earnest. Thinking to himself, he figured he had all the time in the world, and had nothing to lose. *I'll let Asher ramble on. Maybe something worthwhile will come of it.*

"By the way, Daryl, do you like stories about history?"

There was a pause as Daryl thought it over. "You know, Izak—sorry, I mean Mr. Asher—"

"No, no, please stick with Izak. After all, I never think of myself as Mr. Asher. Sometimes when people address me as Mr. Asher, I look around to see who they're talking to. Now that we have become friends, first names it'll be. O.K. with you, Daryl?"

"Sure thing, Izak. My first response to your question is that I never gave history any thought. I've bitterly learned that the here and now is what counts."

His voice suddenly became deeper, with his friendly expression replaced with a resolute grimness.

"Like when I was slogging knee deep in Vietnam's jungle marshes—a Godforsaken place, where—if you weren't paying attention and listening to every sound—you could get your head blown off. It was no time or place for daydreaming.

"But on second thought," he visibly brightened, "I have always been interested in my Apache heritage and enjoyed listening to stories of the old days told by my grandfather. When the guys in my unit heard I was part Indian, they started calling me 'Chief.' I took a lot of good-natured ribbing, but somehow it made me feel special, and I liked it. I even let my hair grow long and tied it into a ponytail, like I figured the Apaches did."

Daryl abruptly stopped talking; turned his head away from Asher; ran his fingers through his hair; looked unsettled; and in a throaty voice said,

"You know, Izak, I haven't mentioned Vietnam in a long time . . . I'm sorry to have gone down what you call a 'byway.' It's a bloody awful one, which I have tried hard to forget."

Asher spoke hastily. "I think for the time being we'll put your stories of Vietnam on hold. Without a doubt they're extremely important, and I vant to hear more about them, but let's stick with the 'Jew stuff' for now."

Daryl nodded in agreement and remained silent, as he composed himself.

Asher paused while he digested the offhand remark about Vietnam. *Aha,* he thought to himself, *that's likely the source of Daryl's pain and turmoil—it goes back to Vietnam.* Asher decided he would encourage Daryl to tell about his war experiences, even though he might be reluctant. Asher knew from personal experience that talking openly about buried troubling memories helps. But he also learned how difficult it was to set aside upsetting reminiscences. *Those damned images,* he ruminated, *seem so deeply etched that I doubt they would ever totally fade.* But, he also was encouraged that with the passage of time they dimmed, and one can learn to live with them. He planned to mention to Daryl that happier more satisfying current experiences tend to wall-off the troubled past.

Asher shrugged his shoulders—a gesture of futility—an implicit acknowledgment of life's insoluble travails. He understood that they both suffered from awful memories, and instantly felt an empathic link with Daryl, along with a burgeoning sense of kinship. *Maybe,* Asher speculated to himself, *if I share my past with him it might help him to release his own terrible story. But for now, good to change the subject.* He then looked directly at Daryl with his warm smile, and said,

"Let's get on with my stories, and start with the—brief—history of Yiddish. Way back when the Jews entered Europe from their homeland in the Middle East, they were basically Hebrew speakers, and likely also possessed some fluency in Latin and Aramaic. As they migrated north of the Roman lands they encountered vast German populations, whose language they slowly learned. The basic German dialect acquired by the Jews also incorporated some Hebrew words—as well as an occasional expression from other non-Germanic peoples. In time, this new language stabilized, to become known as Yiddish, and eventually supplanted Hebrew as the communal Jewish language. A curious phenomenon occurred while the Jews were learning German—they used the ancient Hebrew alphabet (in which they were literate) to phonetically write the German words. The practice took hold and survived. Thus, up to the present, the two fundamentally different languages, Hebrew and Yiddish, are the only languages that use the Hebrew alphabet."

Asher paused, and was pleased to see that Daryl was more relaxed and had been listening attentively.

"Now that I have your attention," continued Asher with a chuckle, "here's your second Yiddish word—boitshik—which I used a few moments ago. One of my favorites. It has layers of meaning, unlike anything in English. It's an affectionate term for a boy or man—commonly used as a friendly greeting by an older person when addressing someone younger. See how your Yiddish vocabulary is growing."

"You do tell good stories, Izak," said Daryl, "but what about this big Jewish holiday that's coming up? I heard one of the guys around the newsroom say it's a Jewish Christmas."

"See, what did I tell you about Jewish byways? Here's one for you. To keep Jews in proper perspective, it's helpful to recognize how few we are—with only a trivial few million within about 300 million, the Jews qualify as the smallest minority in America. Therefore, the overwhelming Christian culture, religious and secular as well, inevitably blinds folks to Judaism. Even with good intentions, most Christians tend to see only a distorted image. And of course, the effort of some Jews to appear more assimilated, and less different, has only complicated the situation. A perfect example of the confusion is what you heard about Jewish Christmas. Simply stated, there is no such thing as a Jewish Christmas. It so happens that a very notable Jewish historic battle—predating the emergence of Christianity by some two centuries—called *Chanukah*, is celebrated around the same time of year as Christmas; and in like fashion, children receive gifts. There the relationship ends. As you know, Christmas celebrates Christ's birth, but Chanukah is completely different—it celebrates an astonishingly successful Jewish revolt against the ancient Syrians. See, Daryl, how enthralled the Jews are in history. Their focus on the past does give considerable substance to Judaism, but I believe it has drawbacks. When highlighting too much of our negative past, which the Jews have a tendency to do, it might tend to cloud people's optimism about the future. Oh my, listen to me going on. Genug is genug ("enough is enough"). Here I slipped in another Yiddish word for you.

"Now back to Chanukah. Additionally, there is more confusion—Judaism utilizes a very old *Lunar* calendar, which is quite different from the universal *Solar* calendar. Therefore, Chanukah falls on different Solar calendar days each year. Sometimes it is very close to Christmas, while at other times it occurs many weeks earlier."

"Izak," offered Daryl, "I'm very impressed how well informed you are about these matters. If it isn't too intrusive, may I ask whether you're a Rabbi? Surprised I knew that title, eh? Can't tell you where I picked it up. Could be in a movie. All I know is that a Rabbi is like a Jewish Priest."

Asher was not only surprised but pleased with the question. He reached across and gave Daryl a congratulatory pat on the shoulder, and while smiling broadly said,

"So, we stirred the pot, and you dredged up something Jewish. How wonderful. I bet hidden down deep in your mind there are some other morsels. Well, to answer your question, yes I am a Rabbi. Or, I should say, I was ordained years ago, but no longer serve in that capacity. Since you raised the subject, allow me to clarify the important difference between a Rabbi and a Priest. The Catholic Priest is the functional intermediary between the worshippers and God. His physical presence and ministry is essential. While, in contrast, the Rabbi is only a knowledgeable teacher. He might routinely conduct a worship service, but it could be run by a lay person just as well."

"Amazing how little I know," Daryl said, with a broad smile of his own. "I warned you at the beginning. But I learn fast. Say, Rabbi, why don't the Jews embrace the Solar calendar like everyone else?"

"Certainly sounds like a reasonable idea," answered Asher, "but since Judaism started way back over three thousand years ago, its religion was firmly established. So when Solar calendar reforms were made—attributable early-on to Julius Caesar, then Pope Gregory in the 1500's—the Jews ignored the changes and kept their Lunar calendar for consistency in religious calculations. Moreover, presumably the old Rabbis back then simply preferred to preserve their well-established traditions, and keep the religion increasingly unique. Like you said, being part Apache made you feel special. Well, using a different calendar than the rest of the world is certainly distinctive.

"Now that we have become buddies, I don't want you to get the wrong idea and think I insulted you back when I referred to your name as being goyish. It simply means someone not Jewish. That places you among the world's 99.99 percent of the people. Maybe even a higher percentage, if we could calculate it. When you write your article, I would like you to consider how a relatively small group of Jews have not only survived horrendous obstacles through the millenniums, but also on occasion gloriously flourished. It certainly might lead one to believe in miracles—or if spiritually inclined, it could be credited to the work of the Almighty."

With his head down, brow wrinkled in concentration, Daryl started to take notes. The thought crossed his mind that his article should have some background material about Izak, and without looking up he asked,

"By the way, Rabbi, where are you from? I mean what country. Are you German, Polish, or from some other place?"

` "Ah, your question, like most issues mit Jews, happens to raise a troubling subject. During the centuries of Jewish life within Europe we weren't treated as a legitimate part of the country we lived in— until fairly recent times. Historically, we were tolerated only within circumscribed limitations: We could not own land; were proscribed from employment in a wide range of basic occupations; and were corralled into designated narrowly confined living areas. Jews were made to feel unwelcome, only superficially accepted, disdained by the majority population, and the Jewish communities were universally viewed as exotic foreign intrusions—not authentic citizens."

The Rabbi paused. His smile had faded and was replaced with a serious expression. Turning to face Daryl, as though sizing him up, he seemed lost in his own thoughts. Daryl sensed the Rabbi was about to say something important, so he waited quietly. Finally the Rabbi gathered himself and said,

"Daryl, what I am about to tell you has burned in my gut for most of my life. It is a painful knowledge which I am unable to forget, and must live with. I think this is the moment to share it, and especially mit you."

Again he paused. He looked down. Nodded his head with determination, and very slowly said,

"I would be remiss not to mention the active role of the Catholic Church in initiating and perpetuating a sustained anti-Jewish campaign for almost two thousand years. The Church's responsibility for labeling the Jews as a 'Pariah people' is undeniable. After generations of European enmity towards Jews, it is not surprising for the climactic German horror of the holocaust to have occurred . . . I wonder, Daryl, are you familiar with this 'sideshow' of World War II?"

"Only superficially. I wasn't born until after the War, in 1950. We heard very little about that period in school, other than we won the War."

Daryl felt awkward. He recognized that the Rabbi's powerful recollections had upset him, and Daryl couldn't immediately think of what to ask or say. The Rabbi also had turned away and seemed involved in his own thoughts. Daryl was only vaguely aware of anti-Semitism, and was startled to hear the Catholic Church was to blame, though not surprised with anything about those Italians. Still, he wondered what they had against the Jews. Finally, the Rabbi turned back, and with a wry smile said,

"I almost overlooked answering your question about where I'm from. You should now understand when I say that the selection of a country of origin by a Jew requires qualification. To be perfectly forthright, most Jews avoid this dilemma, by simply declaring their origin is from a particular country. My more candid historical answer is that I am a Jew first of all . . . who happened to have resided in Russia."

While Daryl made a few quick notes, his attention was unexpectedly interrupted by visions of listening to his grandfather's tales about the Apaches. Momentarily he stopped writing, and puzzled over what had awakened those recollections. With a figurative shake of his head, he brought his focus back to his article. Daryl was delighted at how willing the Rabbi was to talk, which encouraged him to continue to ask about his past. Flashing his best full-toothed smile, Daryl said,

"Rabbi, I'm intrigued with your explanations. Stuff I never heard before. I sure would like to hear about your life in Russia during the big War."

The Rabbi nodded his agreement, and thought how well the discussion was going. *Now's a good time to share my painful past.* He knew his reply would be both unavoidably didactic and somewhat indirect, so he answered as follows:

"Daryl, I recognize that the tools of your trade as a journalist are words. Therefore, I want you should learn that I take strong exception with the popularized media word, *holocaust.* It is from the Greek, literally meaning 'a sacrificial offering to the gods.' Its implication is grossly offensive. By no stretch of imagination can the German industrialized murder of about six million Jews, along with untold millions of others, be rationalized as justified. We prefer the Hebrew word Ha' Shoah—unambiguously meaning, 'calamity or catastrophe.'"

Daryl seemed spellbound by the new subject. He was continuously amazed at where the Rabbi directed his comments. With his pen and notepad held in readiness he hadn't made any additional entries. Noting Daryl's fixed attention, the Rabbi continued.

"When the Germans invaded Russia, they had no difficulty rounding up all the Jews, since they were conveniently settled in separate villages. Along with many others, I was shipped off to the nearest concentration camp in Poland. These camps were the German's bestial facilities for efficiently murdering millions of civilians, and were the awful 'side-show' of the war. For me, it was the war's 'main-show,' as you could imagine. The place was a manifestation of unparalleled evil. One could almost detect the sulfurous fumes of the devil's presence.

"By a thin thread of chance, I survived. Recollections still plague me, and often keep me awake many a night, as I repeatedly relive the harrowing experiences. Implausible as it might sound, my senses have been permanently contaminated by the dreadful odor which infiltrated the camp air from the piles of burning corpses."

The Rabbi took a deep breath as though to clear his fouled lungs, looked around furtively, and continued his story.

"Daryl, you now see a much depleted old man. But shortly after I arrived at the camp and realized the horror of my imminent fate, an uncharacteristic boldness overcame me. I was barely twenty years old, and looked forward eagerly to life. It seemed unreal that it would soon end. Near hysterical mit fear, I imagined a plan for survival. At first it was a mere fragment of a notion, without substance, and quickly dismissed. But time was against me, and I repeatedly returned to this rash idea. As a drowning person desperately grasps a fortuitous floating object, I convinced myself that the plan would vork."

Again he paused. Retelling the painful past had unsettled him more than anticipated. But he was determined to continue. Daryl could see that the Rabbi's usual pleasant, benign expression had changed—he looked older, and his healthy pink cheeks seemed to have faded to a sickly grey. Nonetheless, the Rabbi resumed.

"I remember the day as if yesterday, when I marshaled all my courage and acted on a dubious scheme. When the guards rounded up people and marched them off, they were never seen again. Actually no one was sure of what happened to them. All we had were wild speculative rumors. So the next time the Germans came to collect a group, I boldly decided to follow them.

The guards came soon enough, but at first I was frozen mit fear and couldn't move. If by chance they had selected me, then it would have been the end. Finally, somehow, I settled down, and desperately pulled myself together, and slowly crept out of my barracks. As unobtrusively as possible I quietly stumbled along, just far enough behind the rear guard not to draw attention, while bending over as if I were picking up debris. The Germans were coldhearted killers, but they liked to see a clean place, so I was ignored. My linguistic skills also paid off—I understood German and could converse in that language like a native. My sly maneuver worked just fine. I learned the awful truth about how they killed people—they were gassed to death in a special room. But what really saved my life was what I overheard the guards talking about among themselves. They noticed that the lower edge of the door to the gas chamber didn't seal completely. One guard said it should be reported, but another argued it was a waste of time, that since the gas tended to rise, the door was tight enough. He then reminded them that everyone was always dead when the door was opened. His final statement was convincing. They shrugged their shoulders and moved on. That's when I formed my plot.

Time was against me, and I had to work fast. There was no warning, and I could be selected next. I needed a thin piece of metal, or even cardboard. My plan was to make a small funnel—small enough to hide in the palm of my hand. When the gas chamber door closed, I intended to quickly lie on the floor with my mouth up against the bottom of the door: the tip of the funnel would be inserted into the crack; my hands tightly cupped around the funnel would cover my mouth and nose. With luck I would suck in enough outside air . . . and live."

The Rabbi stopped and looked worn-out. Daryl didn't say a word. He understood that the Rabbi had opened a deep wound, and was best not interrupted. Draining out those foul memories offered hope of lessening their ongoing disruptive impact. Thanks to the Rabbi, Daryl now understood that talking about painful recollections was better than trying to bury them in silence.

The Rabbi forced a smile, raised both hands, and with a voice still choked with emotion, said, "Boitshick, I still can't believe that I survived. One of my worst nightmares finds me on the floor in the gas chamber trying to suck in fresh air, only I'm not getting any. I wake in terror, gasping for breath, and soaked in sweat." There's a lengthy pause, and then to Daryl's surprise the Rabbi started laughing. It sounded hysterical, and before he knew what happened, Daryl joined in. They looked at each other, spontaneously reached out, grasped a tight hug, and then slowly their laughter turned into sobs.

No one spoke for a while. Daryl looked grim. Finally he very softly said, "Yes, Rabbi, fear is something I know all about." He paused, took a few deep breaths and continued with unconcealed bitterness.

"What was the purpose of it all? Sending thousands of young men to Vietnam, only for some fifty thousand to die, and untold thousands to suffer wounds, physical and mental. From the moment I got off the plane in 'Nam I knew I had arrived in a dreadfully foreign place, unlike the world I knew—it unsettled me, from which I never recovered. Your account of the impact of the sickening odor in the concentration camp strangely delighted me, since I too am so afflicted. I was relieved to learn that I am not the only such sufferer. I never mentioned this before, assuming it was due to something weird about me, and I was too embarrassed to talk about it. When I first breathed the foul Vietnam air, it almost sickened me. It was an unpleasant exotic mix of something sweet and musky, with a prevailing odor of fresh sewage. The horrid smell is still with me."

With his head down, and hands out front rubbing against each other as though diligently washing them, he continued talking without surcease. Daryl spoke rapidly, somewhat constrained, but his underlying anger came through.

"Of course, almost being blown up on my first patrol was something that one never forgets. As the new grunt in our squad, I was ordered to be point man. That is, I was first in line, as we slowly wound our way through the dense growth, and struggled with each step to pull our boots out of the soft, moist, clinging soil. Casualty rates on those patrols were high, so the rationale was to put the unknown newcomer in the most dangerous point position. It was a test of his courage and dependability. If by chance he got killed, the sense of loss was less since no one knew him. I never understood why we were sent out into that infernal jungle on a regular basis. Well, here I was sloshing along out front on that first day, so overcome with terror that I feared I was going to soil my pants, when an explosion went off to my right rear. The sound of small arms fire brought me around. I found myself lying face down, with the ghastly remains of bloody body parts all around me. I later learned, one of the guys had stepped on a hidden antipersonnel mine, placed by the Vietcong. When the action ceased, everyone was surprised that I was not only alive, but not even wounded. For some reason, I was congratulated, as if my survival was due to my battle-savvy knowhow. Henceforth, I was accepted. When they learned I was part Apache and nicknamed me chief, it was assumed some cagey Indian instinct had saved me. I soon realized that all the guys were terrified, which explained why they eagerly latched onto the idea that I possessed some magical charm which would protect them. Our collective fear was an unstated reality, but enveloped us all like a clinging miasma."

The Rabbi interjected,

"Fear and ignorance breed superstition, which thrives when alternative supports are lacking."

"Incredibly," continued Daryl with a burst of enthusiasm, "my life was subsequently repeatedly saved by my squad buddies, who routinely began protecting me. They saw to it that I always ended up in the middle of the group, between two of the bigger men who also happened to carry heavy automatic weapons."

Daryl turned to face the Rabbi with a melancholy look, and moved over closer to him as if to confide a private, maybe secret truth, and said quietly,

"From those days in Vietnam, my feelings of discomfort, fear, and being continuously threatened, have never faded, and always are with me."

For a while neither man spoke. Daryl seemed dazed at what he had said, sat silently and stared straight ahead. Finally the Rabbi reached across, as he previously had, only this time he clutched Daryl's shoulder. At first he didn't speak, but as Daryl, who didn't shrug off the Rabbi's hand, slowly turned to face him once again, the Rabbi smiled, nodded knowingly, and asked,

"So, boitshik, you spilled your guts out. Good. Now tell me, how do you feel?"

With a tired and drained look, Daryl wanly smiled back and said,

"Dear Rabbi, I feel as though a huge load has been lifted. Telling you those terrible stories about Vietnam was like unplugging a drain. I feel weary, but somehow I also feel hopeful. It is a strange sense of freedom. Is it possible those Vietnam horrors are behind me? "

"It won't be easy," said the Rabbi, "but you'll slowly be able to live more peacefully with the memories, while enjoying the present and working towards the future."

"One final request, Rabbi. Can we meet once in a while, sometime soon?"

"Sure, Daryl. And we can tell each other more stories. And do I have stories, you wouldn't believe. I bet you do also. And of course, I'll be looking forward to reading your article in the Herald."

"It'll take me a while to organize my material."

Then with a wide grin and an extended hand, Daryl added,

"And I'll have to figure out how to weave in a little Yiddish."

Their simultaneous laughter echoed loudly through the empty park.

Chapter Two

"Boychik, it's been too long," Rabbi Asher enthusiastically exclaimed as he welcomed Daryl with a broad smile and raised arms. Looking up at Daryl from his seat on the bench, the Rabbi continued, "And, first off, I must compliment you on that newspaper article. You got it just right. No doubt readers were surprised with your command of Yiddish and knowledge of the Jewish holidays. Kind of gives you a special journalistic edge. Maybe some might even think you're a Jew? Heaven's forbid! But mit a name like yours, not a chance." With a knowing chuckle he added, "You've got enough on your plate being an Apache, eh?"

Hearing the Rabbi's friendly chatter warmed Daryl, and he smiled in return. As he sat down on the bench he reached out and shook the Rabbi's hand. In the prolonged silence of the greeting, their eye's glowed with pleasure and the two clasped hands seemed reluctant to part.

Finally, Daryl quietly said, "Izak, I've worried about your take on the article.

Your approval means more to me than anything."

The Rabbi remained silent, nodded in response, while his face lit-up with satisfaction.

Daryl continued, "And you should hear my editor. He not only approved the article, but also let it go to press without a single change. He's a tough old journalist, not easy with praise. But his gruff comments—about how his editorial instincts were sharp as a tack and right on target when he hired me—sure made me feel good. Next he almost floored me, when he said, 'Daryl, now that you've got a handle on this Jew stuff, run with it.' I was speechless, not sure what he meant. Just that quickly he recognized my confusion and added, 'This Jew stuff is great. Readers are writing in with questions and praise, and want more of the same. You've got the bull by the horns, so let's see if you can put together a series of weekly articles. We'll put them in the Sunday supplement. You know, Daryl, this could go national. Go talk to that Rabbi friend of yours. I bet he has a million yarns.'

"Izak, how can I take your stories and write them up as mine. That's like stealing. Isn't it?"

Before he brightened up and answered, the Rabbi had slipped into a contemplative reverie. After a brief pause he answered, "No problem, Daryl. For me, that morning bagel, a restful night in the quiet and peace of the Home, and a stroll in the park when the weather permits, are all I need. The world belongs to you and your generation. I am only an observer. The most precious gift you can give me is to listen to my stories. Nothing an old guy enjoys more than talking about the past.

"Now the challenge for you is to write them up as interesting newspaper articles. Make the stories sound true, based on the experiences of real-life sounding people. Somehow try to weave individual tales into the complex historical fabric of the Jewish people. It's not an easy job, but I know you could do it. You see, Daryl, Jews know their own story, but the rest of the people don't. Your readers will identify vith you as one of their own, and understand the Jew stuff when you write about it better than if told by a Jew. Talking about stories, do I have a good one.

* * *

"My son Paul was a hardworking kid, and decided early in life that he would become a Dentist. Since I didn't have much money and helped him as best I could, he had to basically work his way through school. He loved to tell me the story about when he worked for 'Harry the Caterer' during his Dental School years. Like most stories, it has many layers, superficial and deep. I know you'll enjoy it."

In a suddenly soft voice, Izak began The Story of Harry the Caterer

* * *

"'So who is Harry?' asked Paul.

"With a broad knowing smile, Irv answered, "Why, Harry runs the biggest kosher catering operation in Philly. He's the guy you gotta know if you want work. Look," continued Irv in a quieter voice, sounding conspiratorial, "call him up and tell him I sent you. He likes Dental students, so mention we're schoolmates."

"'Thanks for the helpful lead,' said Paul. 'How much money can ya get? Are the tips any good?'

"'Sorry, but there aren't any tips at these catered affairs. The people pay a fixed amount and it's supposed to cover everything, including our salaries. Now, how much you earn depends on whether you get an early or late job. The few early-men, in addition to serving the meal, setup the dining room, help prepare the food, and for which they get twenty-three dollars. Not bad, eh! Late workers just serve the meal and were paid seventeen dollars. Harry is busy as all hell, and runs multiple affairs most weekends. I once booked three jobs on a weekend. Usually I can depend on two. We'll never get rich doing this work, but the money is good and he pays every week. All I know is he must be doing something right to have such a good reputation among the Jews here in Philly. To tell you the truth, I'm amazed how many people still want a kosher meal. Maybe it's become the thing to do: a sort of public display of Jewish loyalty to tradition, by otherwise secular Jews. Oh well, as far as I'm concerned all that kosher stuff is total bullshit. How about you?'

"Paul, who had been absorbing every word, hesitated to answer. Finally, while turning his hands back and forth in front of him, to indicate some ambiguity or uncertainty, said, 'You know, Irv, deep down I totally agree with you. But I promised my mother when I got married I would keep a kosher home. She's old-world Orthodox, and threatened she wouldn't come to my home for a visit unless she was assured of a real kosher meal. To my surprise, my wife Evelyn agreed to follow all the dietary rules. To start with, she couldn't tell traif from kosher, or milchiks from flaishiks. Considering that she grew up with Jewish parents who ignored the religion and were contemptuous of anything to do with kashress, she amazed me how quickly she became a real good balebosteh. We, or I should say she, lives in fear that my mother would show up one day to check out her kitchen. Frankly, when we occasionally go out to eat, we often end up at Beck's seafood restaurant on the boulevard and enjoy a delicious lobster and some oysters on the half-shell. It looks like we have one foot in the past and the other firmly planted in the goyish present. I bet our kids won't even know from kosher.'

"Paul contacted Harry, received a promise of work, and was told to join the waiter's union, since they had exclusive contracts. Besides paying the requisite union dues, they required new applicants to attend the next union meeting where their membership was voted on. Nobody objected to these transient young men: it vas all-win for the union; they collected some money; and these young students never posed any kind of political challenge to the organization and its leadership. Membership in the waiter's union was the essential passport to earn some badly needed money. Their meaningful futures began after graduation from professional school. That one union meeting Paul attended was truly memorable, he told me all the regulars were elderly foreign-born Jewish men, mit thick accents, who didn't speak in conversational tones, but yelled and cursed each other in English and Yiddish. They acted like a grumpy group, but their shouting was only a cover-up. Their lives were hard. With time, the students and the old-timers got to know each other and they became comfortable working side-by-side. In quiet moments the old-timers shared their worries and health problems. Most of them were burdened mit fears that their strength or health would fail, mit a collapse of their chronically fragile financial security. Actually the neophyte doctors provided useful practical dental and medical advice and guidance.

"In return the regulars showed Paul how things were done. Their tone was loud and gruff, but they were helpful. For instance, the first time Paul was told to rose a bunch of radishes he was utterly lost. He turned to old-timer Sol for guidance, who then sounded off in his usual harsh, irritable voice with,

"'You dumb college kids. Don't they teach ya anything in school? How do ya expect to become a doctor if ya can't even rose a radish!'

"In those early 1950's, most of the 'college kids' were married, some mit children, and a few were veterans of World War II. Moreover, they were first and second generation American Jews, working hard towards professional careers, with little money, for which they had to work part-time to make ends meet. The old-timers' response to them were complicated, ostensibly colored in part with jealousy. The comparison between the lives of the two groups was stark: the young men looked forward to fine futures, while the regulars were dead-ended in continued struggle. On the other hand, the students could have been their children or even grandchildren, in whom the more thoughtful might have felt some pride. Maybe they did, but didn't show it. The old-timers were an unskilled, uneducated, immigrant group, doing the best they could, and the effort aged them rapidly.

"Work with Harry was never assured, so they had to call him every week to find out if jobs were available. Nothing was guaranteed. Paul always asked for an early assignment to earn the extra money, but was grateful for any work. By current standards, the pay sounds trivial, but at the time it was significant, and helped make pay-as-you-go possible for many a Dental (along with a few Medical) students.

"One Friday, Leonard, a classmate of Paul's who also worked as a waiter, asked Paul to drive him down to Harry's place in the afternoon, so he could carve an ice sculpture. Leonard was remarkably talented, and was early-on called a 'Jewish Michelangelo.' His ability to carve realistic looking teeth out of wax set him apart—in a class of his own. While the rest of the freshman Dental students sat on high stools at long lab benches doing their modest best to shape teeth from blocks of wax, Leonard sat in the professor's private office carving a full set of teeth out of ivory. Leonard's exceptional ability was recognized early. The Climax Dental Company, a manufacturer of dental products, hired him to upgrade the anatomic accuracy of their celluloid (now plastic) crown forms—his ivory carvings were used to create the master production molds. Climax's crown forms were videly used to shape temporary crowns and large fillings. Leonard's work for the company paid off with a generous check. The new crown forms he helped to create are likely still in use to this day.

"Paul's prized old 1941 Dodge, mit a quirky transmission, always started, but only after coaxing with strategic pumping of the gas pedal coordinated with aggressive engine cranking. Paul figured he got a good deal for only one hundred dollars, even if he had to patch the many rust holes with a special auto repair mastic, and then hand paint the entire car a glossy black cover-up. Actually to close the deal, an old vacuum cleaner was thrown in.

"Leonard directed Paul to drive into the alley behind Harry's catering headquarters, situated in a nondescript industrial building on Broad Street, down towards center city. It was a convenient location, accessible by bus or subway, and on a major thoroughfare with parking lots for cars close at hand. The interior catering facilities filled the ground floor space. Two extensive fully equipped modern kitchens occupied a large area towards the rear: one for making meat dishes; the other strictly for dairy foods—kosher dictated a complete separation of dairy and meat foods. The high standards of cleanliness, I vas told, needed to pass Board of Health inspections or be viewed unfavorably by curious customers, were very meticulously maintained. That was where the food was pre-cooked—to be reheated at the affair site—and all food stuffs were assembled. A huge banquet hall, probably able to accommodate about three hundred guests, filled the rest of the first floor.

"Harry's office was up front, near the entrance. It vas an agreeable room; no decorative frills—strictly business. A solid oak desk faced the door, with a worn leather covered couch against the wall on the right. Additional seating all faced the desk: an upholstered arm chair off to the left; and three wooden chairs with cushioned seats arranged in a semicircle on the right. Harry knew that these meetings with prospective customers often included family groups, so he astutely provided ample comfortable seating. The only adornment on the soft green colored walls was a large colored photo hung right behind the desk, of a buffet table laden mit a sumptuous food display, and a centerpiece ice sculpture of a bride and groom. The picture dominated attention and certainly was shrewd marketing. People loved the ice sculpture, and Harry sold many—at an appreciable profit above his cost of nineteen dollars.

"It was interesting how the crew understood without discussion that a sly smile on Harry's face meant big savings and higher profits when he booked an in-house affair. Yet, it seemed, as time went on and the general economic climate improved, more people opted for grander affairs in upscale hotels.

"Leonard hastened into the building and hauled out a huge block of ice on a cart. To Paul's astonishment, in a few brief minutes, Leonard carved with only a screwdriver and hammer, the image of a young boy, mit yarmelkeh and tallis ("traditional hat and prayer shawl"), bent forward reading a prayer book. The carving was planned to decorate a Bar-mitzvah celebration the following day. As Leonard hurriedly returned the finished sculpture into the walk-in refrigerator, he casually mumbled that he was paid nineteen dollars for the job (which sounded like a lot of money to Paul, when compared to the hours he spent serving a meal for only seventeen dollars). Leonard was an artist at heart, and he eventually became a prosthodontist, where-in he expressed his sculptor's talent by rebuilding deteriorated dentitions with masterfully realistic-looking artificial caps and bridges.

"Harry vas a classy guy. At the time he was probably in his mid-forties. He likely compensated for his height of a little over five-feet, by maintaining a ramrod straight posture, and paying considerable attention to his appearance. He was slim, with a neatly-trimmed thin moustache, and meticulously groomed black hair. Harry had an extensive wardrobe and was never seen in anything but stylish double-breasted, brashly patterned suits with exaggerated shoulders, along with starched white shirts set-off with garish ties. All the employees recognized that Harry didn't indulge in frivolous conversation, or smile very much, was always polite, and never raised his voice even when dealing with the highly emotional, extremely voluble regular crew of old-timers. His manner was consistent: all business, with little tolerance for nonsense, and his determined, rapid step spoke of a fit, but tightly wound, middle-aged man.

* * *

(gossip: 'rumor, report, tattle, or behind-the-scenes information esp. of an intimate or personal nature'—Webster's Dictionary)

"It is unclear where or when the rumor about Harry began, but the continuous gossip among the student waiters that he was connected with the 'Mafia' was titillating and helped fill the dreary hours on the job with distracting speculation. Of course there was no way to prove it one way or the other, and there had been no incidents or questionable events to confirm the suspicion.

"Harry's presence on every job contributed to his success. His personal greetings reassured the customers that all would run smoothly as planned. Moreover, he shrewdly always orchestrated an additional gratis feature, such as an upgraded hors d' oeuvre, or an unexpected ice sculpture, to the customer's delight and profuse gratitude. He knew that success depended on word-of-mouth by satisfied customers. His minimal token additional expense went a long way in happily spreading the good word about his operation.

"But Harry remained aloof with the staff. Interactions and conversations were purely business, never relaxed and personal. They knew what he wanted and didn't have to be told twice. His manner and impact was as a martinet, who with few words exercised control. The unspoken relationship with Harry was simple— be reliable and perform as expected or you would never be hired again. Thus, the catered affairs ran well and Harry was satisfied. The weekly call to Harry about work was brief: did he have an opening; if so, where and when; and critically, was it an early or late job?

"One affair turned out unexpectedly to be special. It had snowed lightly the previous night, and the plows had cleared the main roads, but they remained slippery and the side streets could be a problem. Therefore, Paul's drive to the Adelphia Hotel in downtown Philadelphia was slower than usual, and he unavoidably arrived a few minutes late for an early-man job. He rushed into the banquet hall only to find an unlikely scene—the crew was standing around instead of feverishly making preparations, and Harry was nowhere in sight. Paul turned to Irv who was sitting near the door mit his waiter's jacket hung over the chair's back, and asked,

"'Irv, what's going on?'

"'This affair could be a blowout. The chef showed up drunk, and Harry's in the kitchen with him.'

"Paul vas shocked, and stood dumbfounded. He turned towards the kitchen as angry voices resonated past the double swinging doors—a poor sound barrier. Each door had a small triangular window so waiters could see if it was clear to push the door open. With his curiosity aroused,

Paul wandered over and looked into the kitchen through one of the glass vindows. Facing the door, some twenty feet away, stood the chef with a large carving knife held high in the air. He was a tall black man, of mature but indeterminate age, unmistakably drunk, who unsteadily rocked back and forth, and repeatedly shouted,

"'Harry, ya little fucken Jew bastard, I'm goin to kill ya. Yas, sir, this is it.'

"To Paul's amazement, there stood Harry, his back to the doors, facing the angry chef about six-feet in front of him. The contrast between the two was re-markable—the chef's towering bulk, dressed for work in his white jacket and checkered pants, dwarfed little Harry in all his sartorial splender—only Harry had a pistol in his right hand pointed up at the chef. It looked like a modern-day David and Goliath standoff. When the chef hesi-tated in his tirade, Harry spoke. His cool manner and brief speech had a stunning effect. Harry had to strain his head to look up at the chef as he quietly and slowly said,

"'Listen to me, you big black son-of-a-bitch. If you take one more step toward me I'm going to shoot you through the head to make sure you die. The city of

Philadelphia will give me a medal for getting rid of one more useless, troublemaking, drunken black piece of shit.'

"The scene seemed frozen, hovering on a perilous brink, when the tension began to ease— like the slow release of air from a balloon. The chef's expression morphed from wild ferocity to a sulk, and he brought his free hand up to wipe the drool from his chin, as he lowered the knife.

"Then the silence was again broken by Harry's startling metallic command when he said, 'Put that god-damned knife down—right now!'

"The chef's posture changed into a defeated slump. He placed the knife on the adjacent stainless steel table, and looked away. Harry slipped the gun into his shoulder holster, slid a chair behind the chef, and gently pushed him down onto it.

Then facing the door, he shouted, 'Someone get in here on the double and make a pot of coffee. We got to sober him up real quick. Let's get moving. I'm expecting two hundred and fifty people here soon for a luncheon.'

"Before Paul rushed into the kitchen to make the coffee, he turned to yell, 'The crisis is over. Better start hustling.'

"Predictably, the gossip about Harry's connection to the mob now changed from tantalizing speculation to a (readily assumed) solidly confirmed fact. In those days people believed that besides the police only gangsters had guns. Inevitably, Harry's courage and behavior when faced with a daunting situation turned into legend among his employees, and also spread rapidly throughout Temple Dental School as the real-life drama was retold by the very witnesses. But the question of whether he would have shot the chef remained unresolved. The unofficial consensus favored the scenario that if sufficiently threatened by the drunken chef, Harry wouldn't have hesitated to shoot him, though presumably in the leg, not the head.

"Those with a different take on the possibilities based their argument on Harry's overriding need to prepare the luncheon. They contended that he would have first fired a warning shot, likely enough to have frightened the chef into submission.

"Of course, no one dared to ask Harry whether he was bluffing, or ask the sensitive related question of—why he carried a gun."

Chapter Three

"Hello, Izak. Nice sunny day for being out in the park," said Daryl. "I hope all is well. With your rosy cheeks, you look like a picture of health."

The Rabbi threw his head back and laughed. "Daryl, if you only knew. I'll not bore you mit an accounting of meineh krank-heit. That's Yiddish for 'my sickness.' The doctors say I'm in great shape, but why are there days when I feel geferlech—a wonderful word which means 'awful.' Yiddish offers not only a word, but the word also contains an emotion: a feeling. To grasp its power of expression, Daryl, you will come to understand that Yiddish is a nuanced language, born within the souls of the Jewish people as they thrived, as well as struggled through generations. Yiddish sings mit poetry and joy, but contains an undercurrent of anguish and pathos. See, didn't I warn you that this Jewish stuff is filled with byways.

"I do tend to ramble on, so let's focus on your articles. It's going to be a challenge to come up with a good story every week. Now, since today's story is rather long, maybe you could split it up and make it into a series? What I'm trying to do, Daryl, is give you a variety of stories, which portray the diverse experiences of Jews. Of course, in that way Jews are like everybody else. But keep in mind that the lives of all Jews have been impacted by anti-Semitism, one way or another. It's a distinctive existential issue. When you write, try to weave this painful reality into your tale with subtlety, don't make it the main issue. Farshtaist? Here, I'm giving you some more Yiddish. With one word I'm asking, 'do you understand?'

"Sure thing, Izak. I get what you mean. It won't be easy, but you can be sure I'll do my best. By the way, you'll be pleased with me. I went to the library and took out a couple of books on Jewish history. Like you told me, it's never too late to learn."

"Daryl, you're really going to be some gantseh ("big") journalist. Little by little, as you live and learn—important to be open and receptive to new ideas, while carefully judging their worth—your writing will improve. Words are powerful. They can be literal blockbusters, or have shaded inferential meanings. Good authors know the difference, and most important, are very selective in choices of words. Expect your singular Apache heritage and life-altering Vietnam experiences to influence your work. Don't reject the impact. They are who you are. Your special insights into events and people will mold your writing into something unique: Daryl's special view of the world.

"Genug! It's time for my story. Some of my family was smart enough, or should I say adventurous or bold enough, to leave Russia way back—even before World War I. This is about one such unusual individual.

* * *

The Story of Nathan ("Natan/Nahum")

"It was a dark, moonless night, in a dusty, debris strewn alley, within a cluster of industrial buildings—located among New York City's dilapidated tenements in the aged Borough of Queens. Having secured the factory door mit a huge lock and doubly secured mit two dead bolts, the man turned to leave. As usual, he carried a heavy bunch of keys dangling from a metal ring in his right hand. Unexpectedly, out of the shadows, a group of young men sprang forward, shouted insults, and surrounded him. There intentions at first were unclear, but through the ugly Jewish aspersions and threats of violence, the demand for money became evident.

"It took Nathan a few moments to recover from the unexpected assault in that darkened, lonely place. He stood perfectly still, and failed to fathom their number. But he did spot at least two heavy clubs swinging menacingly in the air, and a bicycle chain wrapped around the raised hand of one tormentor. Like Indians attacking a vagon train, they circled and moved ever closer. Nathan's initial shock and anxiety were soon replaced mit a smoldering anger, as he tried to assess his options. At that instant, he was struck a forceful blow to the center of his back. Momentarily he held his ground, stifling any sound in response to the pain, and then rapidly swiveled to face his gleeful leering attacker—who then nonchalantly turned towards his cheering companions to relish their shouts of praise. Instinctively, drawing on the depth of a life burdened with resentments and repressed rage, Nathan struck back. Mit all his might he swung his right arm forward. Drawn by centrifugal force, the many keys splayed outward, and their crash against the villainous thug's head resonated loudly.

"The cacophony of human voices abruptly ceased, as if a switch had been turned off. The short-lived silence was broken by piercing screams, which were magnified as the sounds echoed off the brick walls in the confined space. The injured thug dropped his club, fell to the ground, and howled mit pain mingled with hysterical weeping appeals for his mother.

"His companions were unmanned: most hastily fled; but one hesitated, looked fearfully at the man, and after he received a nod of approval, went to help his fallen friend. Nathan didn't speak a word. He turned and slowly resumed his walk out of the alley, seemingly unaware that the jingling keys dripped blood.

"'Damn those punks,' he muttered to himself. 'Maybe now they've learned a lesson, and won't bother me again. Why don't they make something worthwhile of their pitiful lives?' He walked for a while, and again mumbled with partially constrained anger, in a resolute voice, 'I didn't travel halfway around the world, struggle and work hard, and finally establish my own business, to have it threatened or taken away by anybody.'

"As was typical throughout the Russian Pale, the small city of Gomel had a sizable Jewish population. Nathan's birth in Gomel in 1887 evoked considerable joy: he was the first born, and as a boy fulfilled his father's fondest hopes—while his mother was considerably relieved that she would not have to deal mit her husband's disappointment if a girl were delivered instead.

"The land mass of Russia was huge, and the Imperial power seemed equally unlimited. Yet, the minority Jewish population was an historical concern to the rulers. So, in response to dubious pressures, political concerns, an inbred intolerance, and possessed of rabid anti-Semitism, the Czarina (Catherine the Great) decreed in 1791 that the Jews were henceforth only permitted to settle in the border areas of the Empire, referred to as the Russian Pale. The Jews were thus effectively forbidden access to the inner heartland of Russia.

"By the time Nathan arrived, this old exclusionary policy was the established law, and was assiduously adhered to. Clearly the Jews had no recourse, and reconciled themselves to this residential restriction as best they could. But the policy caused deep-seated resentment, and made them feel like some sort of plague-ridden threat. Moreover, the consequences of oppressive government restrictions on Jewish employment had inevitably contributed to much Jewish impoverishment. Nathan was keenly aware that his father's career as an attorney was significantly proscribed—officially Jews couldn't practice the law, and were specifically banned from representing clients in court. Despite these restrictions, his father had economically prospered due to an unlikely partnership mit a gentile attorney—whereby he could privately consult with clients, and when required his partner would represent them in court. But this subterfuge with a sub-rosa practice frustrated Nathan's father. He was a proud, intelligent man, who suffered a disquieting sense of humiliation and much repressed anger—which were inescapably absorbed by his son.

"The Jewish population knew they were an unwelcome and barely tolerated group: as if they were offensive uninvited guests. Not only were government restrictions onerous and unjust, but also the dominant Orthodox Christian Church had consistently for generations proffered unrelenting malicious and vicious anti-Semitic diatribes. It would have taken a rare, thoughtful Russian to have resisted this pervasive litany of vilification. For the most part, the Russian population were effectively indoctrinated mit anti-Semitism and complicit mit the prevailing cultural norm—they harbored animosity towards the Jews along with considerable suspicion. Therefore, the general atmosphere for Jews was unfriendly at a minimum and, frankly, was hostile at times.

"And, as if all this weren't enough, the Jewish communities were subjected to threats, that included actual physical attacks on their lives and property by government sanctioned militias—known as 'pogroms.' These attacks erupted in a fury in 1881, spreading fear, death and havoc among the defenseless Jews. Life in Russia had become intolerable. Ultimately, when the visions of a better life elsewhere became palpable, Jews migrated in vast numbers.

"During Nathan's impressionable adolescent years, the rumbles of political reform and revolution had swept Russia. Many Jews had joined the protests, motivated in large measure by the hope that the overthrow of the Czar would usher in a more liberal climate for their people, with the abolishment of all the hated restrictions. Nathan was caught up in the excitement of those heady days. He found a ready welcome among the ethnic mix of agitators, and delighted in the egalitarian spirit. His parents were shocked by their son's involvement in the political unrest, and were particularly fearful he might be arrested for his participation. Russian prisons were notoriously cruel and barbarous, in which inmates often disappeared, never to be heard of again. Nathan's father was especially upset that his eldest son had categorically refused to follow him in the well-established legal practice. Probably like his father, Nathan was strong-willed, self-reliant, and disposed to challenge the status quo.

"Besides aligning himself mit the protesters, Nathan was determined to become an arbetter ("worker"). Since the government's restrictions had forbidden Jews membership in the trade guilds, Nathan appealed to his father for help. Although initially dismayed and disappointed at Nathan's actions, as well as reluctant to further what he viewed as his outlandish plans, he ultimately relented. His father came to accept that Nathan couldn't be persuaded to change his mind, and was determined to follow an alien path.

"With the invaluable intercession of his father's gentile law partner, Nathan was accepted as an apprentice in a small foundry—where a commitment of a monthly financial subsidy (not revealed to Nathan) overcame the owner's reluctance and sealed the arrangement. The dirt, grease, deafening noise, and long hours of ceaseless toil thrilled Nathan. He felt at home in the factory and eagerly applied himself to whatever task he was assigned, no matter how humble, while paying close attention to everything going on. From the very outset, his questions were always appropriate, and he increasingly demonstrated a rapid grasp of the procedures involved. Nathan was a quick learner, and for a Jew, spoke a very satisfactory Russian replete with the usual colloquial expressions and choice profanities—to everyone's delight. He was an eager apprentice who easily fit in socially. The owner along with the men soon lost their initial skepticism about this young Jew, observed how hard he labored, and accepted him as a fellow worker. To an outsider, the unbelievably noisy factory might have seemed a chaotic hellish place—fierce fires blazed, machines roared as though in the throes of self-destruction while belching forth clouds of dark putrid smoke, and in the foundry's darkened bowels brawny, soot and sweat covered men struggled to wrest sense out of stubborn iron. Nathan was daily assigned to assist where needed. He learned how lumps of amorphous metal could be shaped, ground, welded, cut, machined, melted and reformed, and finally polished until a recognizable object was created. This wondrous process of transformation convinced Nathan that his instincts were correct—he had found his calling.

"At the end of each day Nathan returned home with the accumulated filth on his clothes and body as though he wore a badge of honor—to his mother's misgiving. But it was the love of his life, Cousin Esther, to whom he turned to share his enthusiasm. She was orphaned as a baby and brought up by his parents, along vith him. Still covered with dirt, he would run to find her, and breathlessly spill out all his day's marvelous discoveries. She was a good listener, laughed and clapped mit delight at his accomplishments, while continuously amazed with her fearless cousin, whose passion for life seemed like a force of nature.

"Change is inevitable, and Russia was in turmoil. People were organizing, many furtively moved around the country, and most striking were the mass migrations of Jews. They fled in large numbers to South Africa, Mexico, and Canada, with the largest contingent destined to arrive in America. Also, many other countries experienced Jewish immigration encouraged by reports of prospects for a better life from a family member or close friend who had already migrated, Jews packed what they could carry and traveled to strange, far off places.

"The Jews were not the only group on the move, but their world-wide dispersal was most remarkable.

"In Gomel, Nathan was totally immersed in work at the foundry. But circumstances beyond his control were about to change his life in ways he couldn't imagine. The first shock occurred when his father took him aside, and without any preparation told him, 'Esther is leaving for America. Close relatives of ours who have migrated many years earlier, and are now settled securely, have offered to finance Esther's passage and accept responsibility for her care. Furthermore,' he said, 'these plans actually have been in process for many months.'

"With Nathan stunned into uncharacteristic silence, his father concluded with the devastating matter-of-fact statement, 'Esther is scheduled to leave within the week.'

"Nathan was crushed.

"His father, sensitive to his son's reaction, tried an explanation by patiently telling him, 'I am sure you know how life for Jews across Russia has seriously deteriorated. When I received this marvelous opportunity for Esther, I couldn't in good conscience stand in the way.'

"When the day arrived for Esther's departure, Nathan boldly embraced her in farewell. With tears streaming down both their cheeks, they lingered in each other's arms. Before they separated, Nathan whispered, 'I will follow soon.' And she quietly replied, 'I will wait for you.'

"Unnoticed, his mother's raised eyebrows silently signaled her disapproval of such public display.

"After Esther left, Nathan felt restless, and conflicted: he desperately wanted to follow her, but he also was reluctant to give up his job—there was still much to learn. Work filled his days, but as time passed Nathan was upset by his continued struggle mit irreconcilable indecision. The thought of leaving the foundry was made more difficult as his responsibilities increased, along with greater acceptance by his coworkers. He had quickly proved his worth and skill, and had begun to feel part of the group.

"But, he terribly missed Esther, and dreamed of their reunion. While in the throes of uncertainty, events suddenly overwhelmed him once again. This time he would have no choice. Circumstances forced a hasty decision.

"He had been called into his father's study for a private talk, and wasn't at all prepared for what he learned. As he noted his father's pale face and heard the surprising tremble in his usually strong voice, Nathan guessed something terrible had happened. They stood poised facing each other, mit anxiety and tension reflected in their faces.

After a moment his father said in hushed tones, 'I have just been authoritatively informed that the police plan to arrest all protesters. By chance, a gentile clerk in the city's administration building—as I'm sure you are aware, Jews were never employed by the government—happened to learn of the impending roundup. He told the heady news to his Jewish wife, who fortunately, thank God, then urged him to tell me—since you are appallingly on the list of those to be arrested.'

"Father and son silently looked at each other, momentarily overwhelmed with emotion as they absorbed the shocking news, and then suddenly they moved into each other's arms. It was an obvious parting embrace, in which they understood the unstated reality of an inescapable permanent separation.

"There was no choice—Nathan had to immediately flee. The police action was expected within days, if not on the morrow. Time was of the essence. With rushed preparations that same night, Nathan pocketed whatever money his father had on hand, kissed his near-hysterical mother good-bye along with his siblings, loaded a knapsack with bare essentials—and in the dead of night vigorously walked out of Gomel. His mind was in a whirl of excitement. The suddenness of events was unnerving, and he felt the unfamiliar gut-wrenching spasms of fear. Above all else, he was unfaltering in his determination to avoid the horror of arrest.

"He also felt flushed and angry, and mumbled to himself with bitter regret, 'I will sadly never enter the foundry again, rejoice in the camaraderie I so relished, and I can't even leave a farewell message.'

"He followed his father's advice and headed south towards the port city of Odessa, where a distant cousin lived. A letter to the cousin was posted immediately, with an account of Nathan's circumstances, and a request for whatever possible help and assistance he could render.

"It was early fall weather mit balmy days, but the wind's increasing intensity gathered large cloud masses which predictably brought rain. Nathan knew as the days cooled, there would be a promise of snow mixed with rain, then replaced with heavy Russian snowfalls, and finally the likely arrival of blizzards of monumental proportions. He rapidly walked due south, eager to outdistance both the police and the worst of the weather.

"Through her fears, tears and anxiety, Nathan's mother had prevailed in insisting he wear his heavy winter coat and high leather boots. Her wise forethought about the weather would serve him well. In those days, at sixteen years of age, Nathan would be considered an adult. And after those strenuous months working in the foundry he had become uncommonly fit: with nary any fat and well-muscled, which enhanced his self-esteem. Despite the disruptions in his life, and his precipitous flight, nothing had diminished his self-confidence and determination. Once he got over the shock, he started to view the situation as an adventure. Of course, the thought that he was finally embarked on a journey to join Esther thrilled and buoyed his spirits.

"No one at home knew the precise distance to Odessa, but his father's estimate was very close. After all, considering that maps were generally unavailable, people made distance judgments based on the length of time it took between places. Therefore, when Nathan's father speculated it would take about one month for the trip, covering some twenty miles a day, it closely conformed to the actual distance of about five hundred miles.

"In reality it took much longer, for whenever any work opportunities became available, he eagerly accepted. Since most of the jobs were for unskilled itinerant labor, they included some modest, though very welcome, indoor sleeping accommodations commonly in a barn with dry straw for a mattress, and offerings of some precious food. Early on, he, out of necessity, had abandoned the strict Jewish Orthodox dietary rules with which he was accustomed. Hunger was a persuasive force, and before long his sense of guilt faded. When a farmer offered a glass of milk to accompany the treat of a hot bowel of meat stew, he gratefully accepted and enjoyed both together, while he pointedly didn't inquire as to the type of meat. The jobs provided a break from the tedium of travel, as well as pleasurable physical labor.

"At one point in the trip, he happened upon the construction of a large industrial building, and stopped to observe. Anything remotely mechanical fascinated him. He sat down on the trunk of a large fallen tree on the side of the road, and while munching a crust of black bread quickly came to the conclusion that the method of construction wasted a lot of time and effort.

Responding to a sudden impulse, he leisurely walked across to the building site, located the man in charge, and brazenly suggested, 'I know how to construct the roof in half the time you are now taking.'

"His comments startled the foreman, who at first was prompted to dismiss this strange young man. But the need to enclose the roof before the snows came had created considerable pressure, and he recognized that at the current rate it was unlikely they would succeed.

Finally, after a thoughtful pause, the foreman turned back to Nathan, who had stood quietly near at hand, and asked, 'O.K., how would you go about it?'

"Nathan smiled, looked up at the roof where untold numbers of men feverishly worked, scattered all over the structure, in seemingly frantic motion. The sight reminded him of hordes of worker ants. When he answered the foreman he knew it would sound bold and unexpected, but he decided he had nothing to lose.

"'I'll be happy to explain how I'd go about it, but only after you have agreed to hire me to supervise the job, with full responsibility over the men. Of course my pay must be sufficiently generous.'

"The foreman studied Nathan carefully. There was something impressive about this stocky, intense young man who conveyed considerable self-confidence and maturity well-beyond his years. He also took special note of his calloused hands—a welcome sign of one who wasn't a stranger to hard vork. Desperate to complete the construction, already much behind schedule, the foreman made up his mind.

With a broad smile, he extended his hand and said, 'First, tell me the name of my savior.'

"Nathan shook his hand with a firm grip, and with a twinkle in his clear blue eyes along with more of a smirk than a smile, replied, 'Your savior in the after-life is undoubtedly Jesus—but for the here-and-now, I'll have to do. I am known as Nathan. If you prefer, I also answer to the

Hebrew name of Natan, or you could use my family's Yiddish name for me of Nahum.'

The foreman burst into laughter, smacked his hand against his leg, and said through tears of delight, 'Well, Nathan, as a Jew that makes you a distant cousin of Jesus, and I can use all the help from whatever source I can get. It's a deal. Now tell me how you're going to do this.'

"The changes Nathan quickly instituted were remarkably successful. The foreman was thrilled that the roof construction was completed in rapid order as promised, before the arrival of the first snowfall.

"Of course, if viewed from a modern perspective, the changes Nathan made mightn't seem very impressive, and could be thought of as only basic to good planning. But when his time and place were considered—along mit his immaturity and lack of construction experience—his ideas and vision certainly displayed a notable talent for ingenuity, organization, and leadership.

"Progress was immediately evident when he instructed all the skilled carpenters to work at ground level, instead of on the roof. This change alone allowed them to efficiently prefabricate (a novel idea at the time) fairly large sections of the roof panels—the dimensions of which were limited by the size men could carry up the ladders to the roof. Previously, these panels were awkwardly assembled on the slanting roof, which was a slow tedious process, fraught with much delay—pieces of wood slipped and fell, nail buckets overturned, and even precious tools fell to the ground. Now, following Nathan's orders, these rapidly assembled large panels were carried up by a team of (low paid) unskilled men—the savings in wages earned the foreman's smile and ready nod of approval. Carpenters already in position on the roof received the panels and promptly fastened them in place. With a noticeable reduction in workmen on the roof at a given time, productivity increased and accidents were reduced.

"Before long, Nathan learned that the foreman was the owner's brother and lacked any construction experience. He was a nice guy, who liked to nip on his vodka during the day, and allowed the workers to proceed without supervision. This explained the near anarchic situation Nathan encountered.

"Nathan also made an additional strategic change, which all seemed patently obvious—he told the roof waterproofing crew to remain on the ground until all construction was completed (instead of going up each day vith the other workers.) Their presence only added to the clutter of materials and created considerable congestion. Clearly the waterproofers couldn't work until the roofers were finished—so they idly sat around on the roof waiting—getting in the way.

"Nathan ordered them to gather the heavy buckets of black pitch on the ground (a viscous semisolid obtained from the distillation of coal tar, routinely used for waterproofing) along with all their large ungainly tools needed to spread the gooey, messy pitch. They wouldn't go up until after all the roofers, assorted materials, and tools were off the roof. When Nathan finally signaled to begin the waterproofing, and it was accomplished efficiently in record time, the foreman couldn't have been more pleased.

"Nathan was congratulated by the foreman for a job well-done, paid as agreed, and urged to remain with the offer of continued employment. But with a broad smile of satisfaction Nathan declined, and indicated his destination was Odessa, where he was expected.

"Nathan's cousin welcomed him to his modest home in Odessa, and though the greeting was friendly, it quickly became apparent that his resources were limited. But the available bath on Nathan's arrival was a real treat, his first since leaving home, and almost a sensual delight. Then it was followed by a restful night's sleep on a regular bed for the first time in a long time. He realized how he had missed the familiar domestic amenities, yet he was proud of how well he managed to live off the land on his trip.

"If there were any lingering doubts about his maturity and self-reliance, they were dismissed. He had demonstrated to himself that he could manage without his father and family, and was capable of facing the world on his own. Moreover, he enjoyed his independence. But the personal inner attributes he felt he now possessed—enhanced inner strength, fearlessness, and the conviction that he could depend entirely on his own resources—although having served him well; were truly invaluable traits; they proved to create interpersonal difficulties in the years to come.

"Next he decided to indulge in a new clothes outfit, readily paid for from his earnings. In spite of his well-worn, filthy garments having been washed for him, they were in such disrepair that he gladly disposed of them. The heavy winter coat was scrubbed clean, aired-out, and retained.

"Odessa was a large city, bustling mit activity, and likely could offer him ready employment. But Nathan had decided not to linger. His cousin guided him to the docks, where the various shipping firms had offices. It didn't take Nathan long to learn that passenger ships directly to America were unavailable, and the combined costs of alternative routing, with changes of ships, were prohibitively costly, way beyond his means.

"To Nathan's surprise, his cousin suggested an alternative to buying a ship's passage. His business of importing spices brought him into contact with various crew members of cargo ships. He had learned from them that a robust smuggling operation existed—certain sailors would smuggle stowaways onto ships—for a price.

"Confronted with the frustration of being stuck in Odessa, Nathan started to think seriously about the alternative. His cousin, on reconsidering his suggestion, became concerned about the risks and dangers involved, and shared them repeatedly with Nathan.

"Restless and eager to move on, Nathan decided to stowaway, as quickly as possible. With his cousin's help plans were made. The cost was high, but still left him with some money. So, one dark night, Nathan was surreptitiously sneaked aboard a German cargo vessel scheduled for a non-stop trip to England.

"Despite the isolation in a deep corner of the ship, Nathan was sufficiently comfortable. As promised, he was brought food and water once a day, and had a mattress and blankets. He literally lived in his heavy winter coat which helped to ward off the cold and dampness.

"His stowaway guide had been very explicit in his instructions and advice, 'It is likely you will get seasick as the ship left port and began its usual rolling and dipping. Use the head if you must heave. Your room is actually an unused locker, and is conveniently next door to a head. In a few days you will get your sea legs and the sickness will pass. The crew is composed of men from many different nations, so if you happen to encounter someone, smile, give him a robust Russian greeting, and move on as if busy.'

"In his first meeting with the sailor, it took a few minutes to discover a common language. The German first tried his limited Russian, but his vocabulary was so basic and limited that Nathan couldn't help laughing out loud. The obvious connection between German and Yiddish was the link to communication. It was slow going, but worked. Nathan wasn't scholarly, but he had a good memory and remembered his father's story of the origin of Yiddish.

* * *

In those ancient days, following the Roman conquest and brutal occupation of Judea, most of the Hebrews fled. As they spread into central Europe, they eventually entered the extensive lands occupied by huge tribes of Germans. Slowly, out of necessity to communicate, they learned to speak German—it was a basic, practical dialect, which incorporated some Hebrew, as well as an occasional expression from other non-German peoples. The Hebrews—who by then were beginning to be called Jews (the people from Judea)—conveniently used their own Hebrew alphabet to phonetically spell the German words. Ultimately, the use among the Jews of their German dialect became so widespread that it actually supplanted Hebrew as the communal language, and became known as Yiddish. Furthermore, the practice of writing

Yiddish with the Hebrew alphabet permanently survived.

* * *

"Though Nathan was free to wander around and explore the lower reaches of the ship, he was forbidden to ever go up onto the deck. It was regularly patrolled by the Captain's men. Stay below, he was told, and all would be vell. Furthermore, he was assured that as far as the Captain and his mates were concerned, he would never see them. Once underway they remained on the upper bridge, where they conned the ship, and where their private cabins were located.

"When Nathan had expressed an interest in seeing the engine room, the idea of such a visit was vigorously rejected. He learned that the engineer in charge was handpicked by the Captain, with whom he was in frequent voice contact over a direct line from the bridge to the engine room. Next to the Captain, the engineer was the most important man on the ship.

"He was a tough, huge, bearded Pole, of undeterminable age, who ran the engine room with an iron hand, which he didn't hesitate to use to strike a worker he judged a laggard. Moreover, his flagrant use of profanity—an incoherent mélange of many languages, shouted in a powerful baritone voice—echoed loudly, and demanded attention. Crewmen judged the significance of his tirades by the intensity of its volume—shouting and cursing were normal speech, but roaring at decibels above that of the engine meant, heads up, danger was afoot. Unhesitatingly, he had been known to cast a stranger into the brig, confined with iron shackles, when he suspected he was a stowaway.

"Nathan was disappointed but had no intention to risk a visit. He would have loved to see the big coal-fired steam engine that drove this huge steel-hulled ship, and compare it to the small model he worked with in the foundry. His days dragged, and he had explored his confined world to where he could find his way blindfolded. He was bored, and given the opportunity, would have gladly shoveled coal.

"One day, to his delight, Nathan overheard a conversation by a group of men—the ship was about to pass Gibraltar. Even in the backwater of Gomel, he had learned of this remarkable geologic feature. He knew it was a huge limestone promontory located on the southwestern tip of Europe, on the Iberian peninsula, which created the northern side of the storied 'Pillars of Hercules,' with Africa providing the other side. Nathan had been captivated as a child to have learned that since the early 1700's, Great Britain had possessed sovereignty of Gibraltar. They used it as a major military and naval installation, to protect and sustain the sea lanes for their world-wide empire.

"Despite the risk of discovery, Nathan threw all caution to the wind and decided to go up top-side and see Gibraltar. It was a chance of a lifetime that he couldn't miss.

"He closed his eyes automatically at the bright Mediterranean sun, and breathed deeply, sucking in the fresh pleasant smelling salty air, as he cautiously emerged onto the deck. He stood still, only his head and shoulders out of the hatch, furtively looked around, and luxuriated in the profound relief of once again being outdoors and sensing the natural world. His timing was perfect, for there was Gibraltar magnificently looming high off the starboard beam. Nathan was transfixed by the sight and held his breath as the ship slid ever westward on its way to the Atlantic Ocean.

"He wasn't surprised to be caught. But when he was conducted up to the high bridge and brought before the Captain, he experienced a mix of surprise and delight—he assumed they would automatically throw him into the brig, but here he was within sight and reach of the master controls which ran and guided the ship. He looked around hungrily, absorbed all the wondrous sights, while his curious mind invoked innumerable questions.

"The tall Captain, with a neatly trimmed mustache and short beard filled mit telltale grey, whose deeply lined face betrayed his years, stood with his hands in his pockets and surveyed his stowaway. It was obvious that this young man was neither afraid nor intimidated, and the Captain couldn't help notice how his blue eyes sparkled with fascination as he looked around.

"Finally, as their eyes met, the Captain asked Nathan his name in German. Feeling challenged and uncertain, Nathan answered in Russian.

"The Captain shook his head and said, 'Nein. Sprechen Deutsch. ("No. Speak German.").'

"Hesitating only a moment, his eyes unwaveringly focused on the Captain, Nathan answered in Yiddish, 'Gut morgen Herr Captain. Ich bin tsufriden eich tsu kenen. Ich red Deutsch nor a bissel. Ich sprechen Yiddish. Mein nomen hais Nathan.("Good morning Captain. I am delighted to meet you. I speak only a little German. I speak Yiddish. My name is Nathan.").'

"The Captain was pleased with his Jewish stowaway, and with his German and Nathan's Yiddish (which is basically derived from German, though somewhat changed and modified) they sufficiently communicated. The Captain, as a typical pedantic German, repeatedly made corrections to Nathan's Yiddish, and offered instead the equivalent in German. It was a comfortable, yet challenging, exchange, which stimulated both of them. After the Captain learned Nathan was a skilled machinist, he decided to use his talents and let him work off his passage. Nathan was thrilled mit the arrangement as he was put to work repairing the innumerable mechanical defects that had accumulated. Though he slept in his original locker room, he was allowed to eat with the rest of the crew. Between his Russian and Yiddish—which slowly started to sound more German—he managed to talk to the men, and soon regaled them with amusing stories.

"Before he knew it, the ship had docked in London. The sailor who had smuggled him aboard shook his hand in fond farewell, directed his stealthy departure from the ship, and gave him the name of a marine repair shop in the port, run by a German acquaintance, where he might find employment.

"Nathan's stay in England lasted longer than he anticipated. After a year, he had mastered English, had been gainfully employed in that marine repair shop, had learned to enjoy fish-and-chips, and had saved enough money for passage to America.

"His 1905 arrival in America was welcomed by his family with open arms, especially by Esther, who had waited for him, as promised. Within months they were married.

"By the time America organized for the looming European conflict, Nathan was in business with a couple of partners. Their machine shop was busy making popular steel radiator covers and they had recently started making brass beds. Eventually they did get a wartime government contract for thick steel plates which were to be bolted onto military vehicles as protective armor.

"Nathan had come a long way. To say he was content would probably evoke his rebuke. He was a complicated personality, whose basic emotional structure had been formulated long ago in Gomel, and hadn't much modified through the years. Fundamentally, he knew who he was and was comfortable in his own skin, marched to his own tunes, and brought to his new country not only valuable skills, but also a powerful energy which meaningfully contributed to its growth and strength.

Chapter Four

Both Rabbi Asher and Daryl looked forward to their weekly meetings out in the park. When their schedule was interrupted by inclement weather, Daryl, who relied on the Rabbi's stories for his articles, went directly to the Home. He usually found the Rabbi seated in the lounge engrossed in reading the daily Herald newspaper. On one such day, the Rabbi wasn't in the lounge, and Daryl was informed he was under the weather and stayed in his room. After Daryl expressed his hesitancy to intrude on the Rabbi's privacy, he was encouraged to go directly to the room since the Rabbi expected him.

Daryl was surprised to find that the Rabbi's quarters were quite spacious—he entered a comfortable well-lit sitting room with upholstered chairs and couch, with bookcases lining the walls filled to overflowing with books; the bedroom and private bath were in the rear.

To his relief, the Rabbi was seated, fully dressed, facing the door, aglow with a friendly smile, and greeted him in a strong voice, "Daryl, I'm sorry for the inconvenience by having you come to my room. Actually I could get lost in here. It's more like an apartment, except there's no kitchen." The Rabbi briskly added with a chuckle, "Today I did go in for breakfast—never want to miss my favorite meal of the day—but then felt a bisel krank ("a little sick"). Can't say exactly what was wrong, so thought it best to take a lay-down for a while. I told the receptionist—a real mentsh ("a person of worth, one who can be respected")—to send you here if I didn't return to the lounge. Hope you're agreeable to stay for our meeting."

"Sure, Izak. Sounds good to me. . . I'm mighty sorry to hear you aren't well," said Daryl with a worried look. "Maybe we should skip today's get-together. If you're not up to it, I don't want to burden you in any way."

"No problem, Daryl. I'm already feeling tip-top, and visiting with you vill pick me up even more. Now that you're here, look around at my library. Go ahead and browse for a bit. I want you to feel free to borrow any book you like. I'm absolutely sure my gantseh ("big") collection of books on Jewish subjects is more complete than the public library's."

Daryl slowly walked around the room, picked up an occasional book, opened it to the title page, checked the publication date, returned it, and moved on. After a few minutes, he settled into a chair opposite the Rabbi and said, "I never saw such a large private collection of books, Izak, and if I'm not mistaken, you've probably read them all." While trying to control his eagerness to impress the Rabbi, Daryl hastily added, "I notice many look like they are in Hebrew. Of course I can't tell whether they're actually in Yiddish or modern Israeli Hebrew. Or maybe even some texts are in older Biblical Hebrew. Also, after only a cursory survey, I'd say many books are in English." Daryl didn't have to wait long for the Rabbi's enthusiastic response.

The Rabbi clapped his hands in praise and said, "Daryl, your powers of observation are impressive. See how well you've absorbed all the Jew stuff I've thrown at you. No doubt, my friend, you have a tahkeh ("real, certain") scholarship potential. So, I think you're ready for a particular book to start off. My pick will surprise you. It was written back in 1928, but I still think it makes a lot of sense. It's titled, The Island Within, by Ludwig Lewisohn, an American writer, brought to this country from Germany by his parents when he was a child. It is recognized as an important study of Jewish civilization, and includes a rather provocative challenge to his fellow Jews that they should return to their ethnic origins and put away the pretenses of blending in with Christian neighbors. Powerful stuff, eh? It's remarkable how the issues Lewisohn dealt mit are still relevant today. Rarely does a literary work achieve such authenticity, as does his book. You'll learn about the overt, yet often subtle existential conflicts that impact the lives of many Jews. Lewisohn's portrayals are extraordinarily valid—better than anything I could do. I know, everybody has inner conflicts, but in addition to the usual worries, the Jews have some very unique tsores ("troubles, misery")—that have persisted for centuries, one generation after another. In my opinion, Lewisohn created a singularly insightful classic. So, boitshik, here's some heavy stuff for you. There's a copy on the bottom shelf over in the corner. Take it. I think you'll find it's better than my stories. I look forward to your impressions after you read the book. Moreover, gloib mir("believe me") what you'll learn will enrich your articles."

"Sounds interesting. I look forward to reading it. But I must tell you that your Jewish religion is amazingly complex. I've learned that it's really a hidden culture, with much diversity and many so-called byways, as you alerted me a while ago. My understanding of Jews and their religion is still very limited, so I am eager for any in-depth help. Hopefully I'm up to the challenge."

"Daryl, don't think twice. I can tell from your delightful articles that you have talent. They were really well written, captured the readers right from the start, and subtly expressed the ta'am ("flavor, essence") of the Jewish characters. Your future as a journalist is absolutely bashert ("fated")."

Daryl felt at a loss for words. He was embarrassed by the compliments, yet thrilled by the Rabbi's positive opinion of his work. Since their first meeting his increased understanding of Judaism has certainly come a long way, giving him satisfaction and bolstered his confidence as a journalist. Moreover, he was thrilled that his articles were accepted by the editor, and that many readers had expressed approval and interest. But his self-assurance remained fragile. Above all else he depended on the Rabbi's approval. Finally he said, "Izak, I'm so indebted to you for your encouragement and guidance. To simply say thanks sounds hollow and inadequate. But," with a smile and wave of his hand he added, "I have also learned from you that too much appreciation is unnecessary. Your quote on the subject, from the Lebanese poet, Gibran, has stuck with me. It goes something like this: To be over-mindful of a gift is to doubt the generosity of the giver."

The Rabbi silently nodded, smiled, and his eyes filled with moisture.

After a quiet, somewhat charged pause, Daryl asked cheerfully, "Izak, how about it. Are you up to a new story for me?"

"Yes, of course . . . Today's tale is going to be about a young Jewish American boy and his encounter with rural people and their rustic environment. To tell the truth, it was more than rustic. Probably primitive is more accurate. Now don't get me wrong. Primitive is O.K. It's just very different. I know you'll enjoy this one. Everybody likes kid's stories. But of course, by now you've identified the central theme that connects all my stories—it's an assiduous undercurrent. This story won't disappoint you. I'll let you judge.

* * *

The Story of Brut:

"'Say, has any of ya guys ever cut a path through a corn field?' ardently asked Brut while they stood outside the barbed wire fence bordering farmer Gillam's mature corn field.

"The two boys were speechless, obviously didn't know what he was talking about, and, not for the first time, were discomfited by their ignorance.

"Brut enjoyed the moment as the knowledgeable center of attention, and with his open, friendly smile, proudly explained, 'What wez do is run fast as possible straight into the field, knocking down stalks as wez go, until wez come out the other side. It be great fun.' He looked from Charley to Stanley . . . paused briefly, and then shouted, 'Let's go!'

"Without hesitation, they followed him through the fence and plunged headlong into the corn field, whose stalks rose over six feet high—well above the heads of these eight-nine year olds. It was an impulsive, thoughtless reaction, without discussion.

"Charley and Stanley—two city boys— were enthralled with Brut, and were motivated to unhesitatingly measure-up. During each summer's visit to the rural back-country of New Jersey, they were delighted to reconnect with Brut. He was their local friend and leader, who guided them into his world of woods, streams, farms, hills, and hidden trails, along with introductions to the domestic farm animals, and assorted wild creatures.

"The split-second, hasty decision to follow Brut into the field was a reflex. The question of the appropriateness of destroying valuable corn stalks wasn't considered. Hurling themselves into the field was likened to diving into a cold river—don't breathe until your head is out of the water; and keep moving at all costs. The shock immediately awakened signals of alarm in Charley. He was stunned to suddenly find himself entirely alone. Although each boy was separated by only a few feet, the density of the corn stalks created sight and sound exclusion, and in addition the plants formed an overhead canopy that blocked most light. Charley ran as hard and straight as possible, while fighting both his mounting fear of getting lost in the huge corn field, and an increasingly unsettling anxious feeling of claustrophobia. With his heart pumping rapidly and breathing becoming more difficult, he yearned to stop and rest, but didn't dare. In a state of near panic and exhaustion he plunged forward seeking light and openness . . . albeit at the same time, in some calm rational compartment of his brain, he vowed never to do this again.

"Charley first met Brut when his family had purchased a few acres of undeveloped wilderness out in rural New Jersey. With the enthusiastic encouragement of his skilled grandfather, a space was cleared in the dense forest for the construction of a small cabin. One day, early-on during his first summer, Charley was amazed to see three barefoot children slowly walking up their cinder-covered driveway, which ran some considerable distance to the tree-nestled cabin, from the clay-colored, hard-packed dirt Mine Hill road. The oldest was a smiling beautiful blonde little girl, about five or six years old, wearing an over-sized, color-faded dress, along with two younger girls—likely siblings—similarly dressed following meekly behind. Charley was shocked to see them heedlessly walking barefoot on the sharp-edged cinders, and called out, 'Don't the cinders hurt your feet?'

"The group of children abruptly halted halfway up the driveway, looked across at Charley with mixed expressions of surprise and anxiety. Finally, the oldest girl said in a clear voice, with what might be called a coquettish tip of her head, flashing eyes, and broadened smile, 'They sure don't.' Then without uttering another word, the three little girls turned around, slowly walked back down the driveway, and were lost to sight behind the dense foliage as they turned right onto Mine Hill's dirt road.

"The girls' cautionary venture up the driveway to check-out their new neighbors was soon followed by their older brother, who came on his own for a visit. It turns out he wasn't much older than Charley; had a lean structure; long, good-looking narrow face, which promised a handsome adult; but had an overly-long neck, giving him a half-a-head height advantage. His denim pants and long-sleeved shirt were well-worn, but looked clean, and his ankle-high, heavy-duty shoes were in good shape, though dull and scuffed from much wear—seemingly never having benefited from shoe polish. Basically, he made a nice appearance—a typical rural country boy with a disarmingly relaxed manner and welcoming friendly captivating personality. In marked contrast, Charley's family had a serious demeanor, especially when coupled with his mother's overriding pose of formality (ingrained from her career as an urban school teacher). Also different was Charley's stocky build with wide cheek bones, inherited from his Eastern-European Jewish forebears. The boy reached out, they shook hands, and he introduced himself as 'Brut.' When questioned by Charley about his unusual name, the boy hesitated a moment, then smiled widely and said, 'My real name be Francis, which no one uses, and Brut, which all calls me, was short for brother. How's about yurself? What is it you be called?'

"They became staunch buddies almost from that moment on. In a way, Brut became Charley's mentor—from which Charley was profoundly and permanently enriched by the experience.

"Brut's world and family were extraordinarily different from anything Charley had experienced. But he wasn't put off, and instead was fascinated and attracted. It was summer freedom time which Charley relished like any youngster, and he thrived in this awesomely different rustic place—to which he impatiently hungered to return each summer. Moreover, Charley easily felt comfortable in, what was to him, Brut's exotic surroundings, and had no difficulty interacting with Brut's family members.

"But Charley thought Brut's very small one-story house was a wonder, and he couldn't imagine where there was sleeping room for his large family. Moreover, its condition was deplorable and looked starkly neglected with peeling paint and filthy windows. The cluttered, dusty, dirt front yard and badly eroded driveway were devoid of any flowers or plantings which could have added some color and cheer. Charley couldn't help conclude that the drab looking house and property unfortunately closely mirrored the circumscribed existence of the inhabitants.

"When Charley walked down the road to Brut's, it was as though he entered a different world—an alternate dimension in substantial reality as well as in character and quality of life. The relatively primitive living conditions of the Birch's—though it lacked most modern material possessions, and were eminently free of sophisticated pretenses—nonetheless, were appealing to young Charley. At his formative stage of life, the dramatic contrast in their lives from his own engaged him. During those summers, spending his time with Brut and around his home, he enjoyed a subliminal identification with them, and experienced a sense of relief from his family's high standards and persistent concerns for his future. Charley thrived.

"The location of Brut's home, just a short walk down from Charley's cinder covered driveway, made for physically close neighbors, but the families were otherwise vastly dissimilar. Charley's family were urban middle class Jews, who esteemed education, and were worldly sophisticated; while the nominally Christian Birchs (Brut's family) were poor rural provincials, basically uneducated, whose world vision was narrowed by overriding personal concerns, focused on immediate basic needs.

"Somewhat surprised, though also relieved, Charley learned that Mr. Birch was gainfully employed. With little or nothing extra for personal enrichment, his income seemingly only provided for a marginal existence—just above dire poverty.

"On a lighter side of the Birch's lives, their radio, always loudly tuned to country music, filled the spaces in their home, and echoed outdoors. The voices of high-pitched male tenors dominated. The lyrics, marvelously repetitive, invariably lamented lost and unrequited love, and were sung with a stylistic twang (a sound new to Charley, which he would subsequently always associate with Brut). To

Charley, the music had a novel plaintiff quality, which he decided must speak meaningfully to the Birchs.

"After a while, Charley got accustomed to the music, and found the singer's crystal clear,   audible articulations of the lyrics both refreshing and engaging.

"As Charley became better acquainted with the Birchs, he realized the extent to which they were emotionally closed-down and very private. He learned to understand that they kept their inner thoughts to themselves (so different from his compulsively loquacious family); seldom offered an unsolicited opinion or critique; and commonly maintained only cordial relationships with outsiders. Yet, to their credit, the Birchs admirably tolerated their difficulties and limitations with seeming equanimity and stoicism. Charley figured the music probably resonated as an important emotional outlet for the stress and sorrow they couldn't articulate.

"Brut, in like fashion, also never vocalized complaints about anything; nor ever made any critical or even laudatory comments about his family; and was generally closed about his own feelings. But, in all encounters with Charley, his mood was consistently cheerful, always eager for a new exploration. Even as a youngster,

Charley was more thoughtful and serious than expected from someone his age. Therefore, it wasn't surprising for him to eventually imagine that the Birch's lives were as if encumbered by a grey miasma, narrowing their existence to a perpetual struggle for survival—their crippling myopic focus blinded them to influences and possibilities outside of themselves. Yet his admiration and fondness for them remained undiminished.

"What Charley didn't grasp at first, was that despite all the negative superficialities, the Birchs not only had strong loving family relationships, but also were capable of displaying an unfettered generosity and friendliness of spirit towards others—with Charley a grateful recipient. Typically, whenever Charley unhesitatingly came to the back door looking for Brut, Mrs. Birch—who was the most haggard, wasted woman he had ever seen—always greeted him warmly, while she busied herself over the large cast iron wood burning stove. Her painfully thin face, bulging eyes with dark circles of fatigue, spoke volumes of the price she had paid for a very difficult life. Clearly, the drain of birthing at least ten surviving children (apt to have been one-a-year; with maybe a miscarriage along the way; and likely coupled with the tragic death of a baby), had taken its toll. Yet, her customary grim expression never failed to immediately brighten with a broad smile when she greeted Charley. Her practice of offering a tasty homemade cookie was a generous and gracious act. Sadly, this middle-aged woman, with a skeleton-like appearance, had lost all the blush of healthy vitality, and looked depleted and elderly . . . well-beyond her years.

"Charley never inquired about indoor bathing facilities, which maybe didn't exist. The single-seated outhouse, setback a short ways in the rear yard, obviously provided for the toilet needs.

"High-spirited camaraderie characterized Brut and Charley's relationship. The lure of the boundless forests punctuated by expansive fields and meadows, which spread out rolling in all directions, much still gloriously undisturbed in the pristine glory and feel of earlier days, drew them to constantly wander and explore. Though Brut was most often the guide, at times Charley's enthusiasm drew them to places Brut hadn't been. Charley could never get enough of his unfettered freedom to discover new and intriguing places, which energized Brut to more widely explore his word than ever before, while at the same time he inescapably absorbed Charley's excitement. It was a dynamic symbiotic-like interaction from which they both thrived.

"Charley was deeply moved by this refreshingly beautiful natural environment, in which he felt at home and unquestionably secure. One day, while hiking across a meadow with Brut, to his surprise he experienced a stunning sense of exaltation, which he never felt before. After a while he was able to generate this marvelous elation by simply gazing out across an open field into the remotely distant forests and hills. It was a private inexplicable joy which he couldn't explain or describe, and never shared with anyone, including Brut. The experience had a positive lasting impact. For the rest of Charley's life he was imprinted with his summer memories to the extent that he regularly spurned cities, and found comfort living out in, what he liked to refer to as, 'the lush rural provinces.'

"No hike or climb was too difficult for these boys with their inexhaustible energy, especially the irresistible attraction of climbing an old wild crab apple tree, where its ground-reaching branches offered easy access. These fairly low growing trees with wide, spreading, thick limbs, so different from their abundant tall stately deciduous and evergreen neighbors, were scattered here-and-there often standing alone—likened to hardy survivors of a prehistoric past. The rewards for a climb were the small ripened, hard, tangy apples that were abundant during the summer months. Despite the caution that eating these apples could cause a bellyache, Charley never hesitated to eat one or two when thirsty and dry, without ill effects.

"One day, Brut led Charley along a narrow path they had never traveled before, which paralleled the 'crik' downstream. It flowed at the bottom of the grade below Brut's house, crossing under an ancient bridge on Mine Hill road. After a brief walk down the path they came to a small pool where the stream had widened. The cool, free running water, a little over a foot in depth was a thrilling discovery. Charley became excited and energized. He decided to improve the pool, and envisioned how he and his family could bathe and refresh themselves. With Brut's willing help, following Charley's lead, they set about the task. By adding stones to the already accumulated large boulders positioned at the downstream end, more water backed-up and the pool was deepened.

They also cleaned the pool by removing rocks and debris, which uncovered a firm dirt bottom pleasant to step on. Before long, Charley's family, dressed in bathing suits with bath towels over their shoulders, regularly walked down Mine Hill road to spend time at the secluded, tree-shaded 'crik' pool. It became a favorite place for folks of all ages. Charley and Brut splashed around in the pool—too small in which to swim—while the adults restfully sat about on the large stones and socialized, after a refreshing dip. During hot summer days, the 'crik' pool was a frequent destination. Charley relished the well-earned praise and congratulations he received for discovering and improving the pool; which was popular with both family and their frequent guests.

"For these urban-bred folks, the little 'crik' pool was an enchanting, unsophisticated, reclusive place, which they immensely enjoyed, and tended to fondly recall through the years. It was a refreshing change from their routine-ized, hurried, stressful lives. The pool's natural surroundings and ambiance—physically shut off from their worldly contacts, and psychologically relaxing—was a joy and delight. The rustic summer cabin out in the woods, with the unspoiled, accessible pool, provided a timely refuge from the worries and turmoil of the worldwide, economic depression of the 1930's, along with the fear and angst caused by the widespread vile anti-Semitism of the times.

"Curiously, except for Brut, his family never went to the pool. It was as though it belonged to Charley's family, and others weren't welcome. This also held true for Stanley—the other Jewish city boy—whose folks stayed at a nearby old farmhouse each summer. Though Stanley often accompanied Charley and Brut on their wanderings, he told Charley that, "I feel the 'crik' was your family's private place, and I didn't want to intrude." Charley did not argue with Stanley since he agreed with him, and his comments also fueled Charley's imagined ownership of the pool. Furthermore, his rationalization that, 'if used by too many people, it could easily be destroyed,' added additional justification to their exclusive use of the pool.

"During the succeeding summers, Charley and Brut resumed their friendship as before, with the long intervening school year hardly impacting. They picked up where they had left off. For Brut, Charley's arrival brought renewed energy to his otherwise colorless life; while Charley simmered with excitement over his return to the country.

"Still, unanticipated events would prove disruptive. It has often been said that life is like the business cycle: it has ups and downs. This was something Charley was to painfully learn, and not once, but three times.

"The first 'downer' was a fairly minor episode, but opened psychic wounds in Charley. He and Brut were exploring along the downstream meanderings of the 'crik,' when they encountered two teenage boys. They vere big for their age, had an imposing unfriendliness which they took no pains to hide, while they puffed away on cigarettes. The lack of greetings alerted Charley that this could be trouble, especially when he sensed how tense Brut had become. To Charley, the surrounding air had suddenly become as if charged with electricity, portending an imminent storm. As they all silently stood looking at each other, he further imagined a dangerous confrontation was about to take place, and he felt helpless to prevent it. His stomach knotted, and his mouth went dry, and even if asked to speak he knew he couldn't. The sustained scowls of disapproval of Charley by the teenagers washed over him with implied threat. Finally in an angry, menacing tone, the silence was broken, when one of them said, "Hey Brut, how come ya got the little Jew kid with ya?"

"Charley was frozen with shock and concern as he glanced at Brut, who after a few moments hesitation and with downcast eyes, plaintively answered, 'Aw, come on now, he's all right.' It was clear that Brut was in a situation over his head, and completely cowed. An ominous silence once again prevailed. Charley's anxieties mounted—he felt exposed and vulnerable and had trouble breathing. The two teenagers stood glaring at them, as if unsure of what to do next, and the threatening tension was sustained. Finally, after what seemed ages, they looked at each other, pitched their cigarettes into the stream and, with dismissive leers at Brut, turned and left.

"Neither Brut nor Charley spoke as they watched the boys walk away. The entire episode had taken only a few moments, but its impact was profound. Charley's heart continued to beat rapidly, and he was sure he heard its sound echoing in his head. As his world slowly tried to resettle back to normal, a deliriously welcome sense of relief washed over him, but never again would it be quite the same. The rustic country that he loved and had learned to know so well had irreparably changed—it now possessed hazards he hadn't anticipated, with some people who rejected his presence as an unwelcome, disliked intruder. It was a sobering experience for a young boy.

"What also saddened and disappointed Charley was his recognition that stalwart Brut had been frightened, and significantly diminished. Never again would Charley look up to him in the same unqualified way as in the past. Without a word of discussion, they turned, walked to Mine Hill road, and went to their respective homes. They continued their daily exploits, but the reality was different—Charley's sense of security and belonging (primal emotional needs; the loss of which impacted him for many years) had been shattered, and replaced mit an uncompromising wariness.

"The days passed uneventfully in a pleasant bucolic haze, as the memory of the upsetting encounter faded, and Brut and Charley's easy relationship was restored. As fate would have it, something unusual happened—one day as the two boys lounged outside Brut's house, a 'downer' again inexplicably germinated.

"Mr. Birch offered to take them with him on a trip to Picattinny Arsenal where he was employed. He said he had to pick up someone, and that the drive would only take about 30 minutes. It was the first time he had ever asked the boys to join him and without hesitation they enthusiastically jumped at the chance to ride in the open bed of his pickup truck. It was a thrilling ride, as they hung on to the side rails, with the air blowing in their faces, whipping up high spirits, as one would on an exciting roller coaster ride.

"The man waiting for them was a stranger to Charley, and as he climbed into the cab's front seat he glanced back at the boys with disapproval and anger. Even before he spoke, Charley once again recognized the awful enmity directed towards him, and froze in fear. The stranger then loudly barked at Mr. Birch, 'How come ya brought the damned Jew kid along?' One moment Charley was remarkably happy, and the next everything shifted as joy vanished. But wondrously, the dire impact was mollified by Mr. Birch. He promptly dismissed the question with an impatient and firm response, which silenced the stranger. Nonetheless, Charley's pleasure in the return ride had been crushed. When they got back, he silently jumped down from the truck and went home.

"This 'downer' had an unexpected 'upside.' Henceforth, Charley learned, in addition to black and white—good and bad—that life had grays. He also knew he would be forever in debt to Mr. Birch. His rebuttal of the stranger's overt anti-Semitism had given Charley a more balanced view of Christians—not all were haters, and some even rejected the popular detestation of Jews, and could find space for compassion . . . as had Mr. Birch for the feelings of a young boy.

"Brut and Charley never discussed the ride. The issues at stake were profound, and neither youngster was equipped to deal with them. For Charley, his upset was personal and he instinctively shut down and couldn't talk about it. Brut, a surprisingly empathic boy, recognized Charley's hurt, but his background had instilled the rule to never intrude in the business of others—look away and move on.

"Brut relished taking Charley to new places, and this time it proved to be really special. With his usual broad smile, he refused to explain where they were going, only to say, 'Follow me and yur going to

be surprised.' On this occasion, he headed to the left of the Mine Hill road bridge,
didn't cross the 'crik,' and kept to a well-
defined but narrow tortuous trail, which
stayed in the valley between the hills.
Charley silently followed along, as was
their custom, with mounting excitement as
he wondered where they were going and
what was so special. After a good twenty
minutes, the path suddenly opened out of
the trees and dense undergrowth into the
bright sunlight to reveal an old, empty
swimming pool. Charley couldn't believe
his eyes, and there was Brut almost bub-
bling over with uncontained laughter. He
said, 'Charley, didn't I tell ya it be special?'

"It vas a large, poured concrete pool,
devoid of water, and partly filled with dirt
and sand. Brut thought the abandoned
pool had been built by a wealthy, long-
departed family by the name of Snow.
Charley's imagination once again whirled
into action, as he walked around the
pool's concrete apron envisioning how
great it would be if they could clean it up
and somehow refill it with water. Why, he
thought, they could actually dive and
swim—a major upgrade from the 'crik'
pool. Just looking at Charley, Brut knew
he was excited, and felt good that the 'spe-

cial' had been a hit. In addition, he wasn't surprised when Charley suggested they get shovels and clean it out. Brut was always game for a challenge, especially when posed by Charley, so they enthusiastically undertook the tedious job. After a week of steady work, the pool was cleaned out, and they were relieved that no cracks or defects were uncovered—the pool was ready for water. But how to do it, they couldn't imagine. So, when they returned to find the pool filled with water, they were thrilled, but puzzled at how it happened. Their best guess was that the removal of dirt from the pool had unplugged the ingress opening, which allowed the water to enter from a hidden spring. They smiled at each other, shrugged their shoulders, and fully clothed jumped into the water. It vas irresistible. They laughed and swam, marveling at the wonder of how the pool filled, while extraordinarily pleased with themselves.

"Charley was literally ecstatic, and wanted to share this new development. The only adults around at the time were his elderly uncle and aunt who had arrived for a visit. Unable to contain his enthusiasm, he persuaded them to join him for a trip to the swimming pool. Though they were reluctant at first to go on what sounded like a rather long hike to get there, they eventually agreed, not wanting to disappoint their nephew. What happened was the worst and most traumatic of the 'downers.'

"After a rather slow hike, Charley's excitement finally couldn't be restrained any longer, so he bolted ahead and called out over his shoulder, 'Here we are. Just up this little grade and there's the pool.' The shock of what he encountered as he came dashing out of the trees into the sunlight stopped him cold, as though he had run into a wall. The pool was packed with innumerable local kids of all ages, none of whom he knew. *Where did they all come from, and how did they find out about the pool,* were questions that flooded into Charley's mind. Standing dumbfounded, trying to fathom events, he suddenly heard a loud voice call out from above, 'Hey, Jews, we don't want ya here. Get out.' He looked up and saw a teenage boy, who alarmingly resembled one of the hostile boys they had previously encountered, sitting in a tree overhanging the pool from which he apparently planned to jump into the water. Charley looked around to see his uncle and aunt standing in frozen silence just in the path opening. The call for the Jews to get out was repeated, which sounded even louder since all the noise and activity in and around the pool had ceased. Out of the blur of the crowd, Charley spied Brut standing silently immobilized, staring back at him with a painfully guilty look. Charley knew at that moment that the news of the rehabilitated pool had to have been spread by Brut.

"Charley turned to follow his relatives back down the path. Stunned and humiliated, his increasing anger and frustration almost choked him. Not only was he upset by the anti-Semitic attack, but the clear injustice of the situation fueled his deep-felt emotions. After all his hard work to clean and restore the pool, he had been viciously excluded from its use. Frustration at his inability to respond stimulated a profound bitterness—both towards the taunter and at his own weakness. He felt diminished. In addition, he felt terribly guilty about subjecting his aunt and uncle to such awful abuse.

"This 'downer' had taught him an important lesson in the way of the world—right alone does not assure justice, but one must have the might to insist on it. It was a truth he wouldn't forget. Moreover, Charley never again went near the pool.

"Some days later, Brut came to find Charley. He was unusually subdued, offered no excuse or explanation about the pool event, but instead quietly asked, 'Why wuz ya so upset about being called a Jew?'

"It was a good question, which Charley found difficult to answer. The issue was complicated and a stretch for a youngster to deal with. He might have wanted to launch into saying that what really hurt was the personal rejection and hatred. Charley's youthful heart had been broken and he yearned to ask, 'What had I done to deserve such dislike?'

"Incredibly naive, but trying his best, Brut then said, 'Call me a bad name. It don't matter.'

"Charley still withdrawn, and uncomfortable with the direction of the conversation, didn't know what to say.

After a while, Brut added, 'I think me family be Dutch. Why doesn't ya call me a dirty Dutchman?'

After a long pause, Charley smiled at Brut's efforts . . . and said, 'Aw, come on you dirty Dutchman, let's go for a hike.'

Chapter Five

Wearing an old hat, and what looked like a nondescript army issue field jacket, Daryl doggedly walked through the rain on his way to the Home for his weekly visit with the Rabbi. Suddenly, unwelcome visions of similar dreary days back 'In-Country' flooded his consciousness, along with how he hated it when the awful jungle muck sucked at his boots. He was from the dry Mid-West, where the ground was solid and secure under foot, so when he was gripped by the mud it felt threatening, as though a malevolent spirit was trying to suck him into its soft embrace. Unbidden, these deeply buried feelings from his anxiety filled army tour in Vietnam had reawakened—he became alert, wary, and tense as he cautiously looked around the near empty streets.

One part of his brain had been aroused to danger, while rational awareness fought for control. He accepted these periodic mental struggles as a sort of handicap, but hoped the nightmarish intrusions would eventually be suppressed. The gradual fading of the flash-backs as his journalistic career happily took off, was encouraging.

So this unexpected reappearance stunned him.

He felt increasingly weary and depressed. His legs became burdensome and he stopped walking. His mind was spinning with conflicting images—pride in how he had turned his life around offered reassurance; but fear that he hadn't the strength to carry on made him feel heavyhearted and pessimistic. The old self-destructive alcoholic yearnings seductively emerged, to which he dallied with the idea that a 'quick one' would fix him up. Yet, he didn't move.

Immobilized, he struggled to overcome his indecision and regain a positive sense of purpose and energy. It was clear that his future was at stake. Finally, as though suddenly inspired, he cried out in anguish, "Good lord, the Rabbi would be crushed if I didn't show up. It would be a terrible way to repay his good-hearted help with my job, and the generous investment of himself. Also, he would surely be devastated if I arrived foggy with booze."

Daryl knew in his heart that if he disappointed the Rabbi, he couldn't live with himself. Finally he drew on the immense inspiration and hope offered by the good Rabbi's recovery from the horrors of the concentration camps. Daryl said to himself, "If the Rabbi survived sane and productive from such an abominable experience, then I have no excuse." Daryl shook his head from side to side, beat his right fist repeatedly into his left palm until it reddened and started to swell, and then with determination resumed his walk—almost at a run—to the Rabbi, while focusing on the anticipated pleasure of hearing a new story.

* * *

The Rabbi smiled broadly and waved Daryl to a chair he had pulled over in anticipation of his arrival. As usual, when they met in the Home's cozily expansive lounge, the Rabbi had chosen a remote corner where they would be undisturbed. The Home's personnel and residents understood these were private meetings and politely did their best to avoid interruption.

"Welcome, Daryl. Good to see you again. You know, if for any reason you can't make a get-together, simply call and leave a message. The folks here are real message mavins ("experts"). By the way, you look a bissel farmisht ("a little mixed up emotionally, befuddled"). Probably due to the ugly weather. Not unusual. Did I ever tell you about the day I arrived in America? As I stood on the dock totally farmisht, it was raining so hard that I thought God was trying to wash me back into the ocean. Not only was I alone, had no relatives, couldn't speak the language, but it was pouring like when Noah built an ark. If it weren't for a kindly little Yiddisher lady from some Jewish welfare group, who came along and took me by the hand, I don't know what would have happened to me. Genug! Vo den ("what's new"), eh?"

"Shalom, Izak," said Daryl. "Just seeing you again, cheers me up. And I love to hear those Yiddish words. I'm really not too sure why. Possibly because it's such a basic part of you. Yiddish links to your rich old culture, as is true of all languages, but unavoidably also invokes its mournful memories—particularly, recollections of historic tragedies. As you sadly pointed out, Yiddish fluency in contemporary days is slowly fading. Curious how knowledge of my own heart-rending Apache heritage, has elevated my sensitization to the sad stories of others. I wonder whether our remarkably similar painful histories might unite us as some sort of very distant cousins, only separated by time and space. Yet, I have also learned that Yiddish speaks eloquently of how both you and many of your people have survived and are flourishing. The wheels of fortune keep revolving. May the sun's recuperative power warm your lives again."

The Rabbi was deeply moved by Daryl's comments. His eyes sparkled with moisture and he was momentarily at a loss for words. Daryl's compassionate tone and perceptive insights evoked joy and gratification. Finally he said, "Boitshick, you've made my day. See! What did I tell you! Once you started writing, your impressive talent for expression, poetic-like no less, would be revealed. You are a natural. Furthermore, you have a rare empathic capacity, which allows you to see beyond the surface of events, and to penetrate the cloud of human emotions. Thus, your journalistic renderings bring a special sensitivity to your work. Fortunately you have an experienced, astute editor who recognized this talent and encouraged you—truly a mitsveh ("good deed").

"Now, Daryl, how about telling me a story today. Something different for a change. I know nothing about your Apache people, and would love to hear their story. And don't skip over any stuff about your background."

Daryl was taken aback by the Rabbi's suggestion and looked away, deep in thought. When he turned to face the

Rabbi, he slowly shook his head, ran a hand through his hair, and said quietly, "Izak, I don't think I'm up to that. First of all, my Apache knowledge is very sketchy. Besides my life has been pretty drab."

"No life is uninteresting, Daryl. Since we've become such good chavairim ("friends"), I would like to hear some Apache stuff for a change. Genug mit the Jew stuff for now."

* * *

Daryl's Apache Tale:

"To begin with, I read 'The Island Within.' Though it dealt with Jewish social assimilation, I can see why you thought it would interest me. Ludwig Lewisohn's concern, in part, that Jewish intermarriage risked dilution of cultural identity, really is a universal phenomenon. As usual, you were right. The issues resonated closely with the experiences of my Apaches. Actually, I believe it boils down to individual choices. The struggle for preservation of a person's special ethos—the complex of ideas and beliefs—is continuously challenged by their relevance in a difficult and changing world. Loyalty to the past unavoidably comes into conflict with needs of the present."

Rabbi Asher raised his eyebrows, then tipped his head, and puckered lips while nodding vigorously—gestures, better than words, which expressed his agreement with Daryl's redaction of the basic issue. His beckoning hand wave further signaled him to continue; while thinking to himself how terribly close Daryl came to destroying his brilliant mind. *It would have been a real shandeh* ("shame").

Daryl nodded back with an appreciative smile and resumed. "Take my family for instance. My father was one hundred percent Apache, and my mother was an indaa ("white") woman. They were drawn together by chance here in expansive America; each responded to the need for love's comfort while they adjusted to the reality of the world around them; and toiled to find a productive place for themselves. It wasn't easy then, and from my limited experience, continues to pose a considerable challenge for many."

Daryl paused, collected his thoughts, and continued. "I'll start with my father ("shitaa" in Apache). As soon as he graduated from the Indian Bureau high school, he took off on his own. Interesting how some Apache words have come back, though that's all I can expect since I never could speak the language. As you would imagine, English was all I heard at home. Both parents worked hard at accommodating the other, with partial success. The net result was an unbalanced blend of their two divergent cultures, with an unsurprising significant loss of the Apache content. In a way we became more American—part of the national trend of cultural homogenization of all the disparate contributions. It just happened. My shitaa went with the flow. I got the impression he was both relieved and comfortable to have moved into the English-speaking world. Our family's experience likely typified many others, especially with mixed couples.

"Somehow, my shitaa eventually found consistent work out in the oil fields as a roustabout. It was perfect for him. His willingness to work hard, and ability to learn quickly, proved his worth to employers. In addition, his inherited robust Apache physique served him well. Oil well drilling needed strong men who could manage the heavy, massive, equipment. He became highly skilled, was frequently called out for jobs across the country, and though the nature of the work didn't provide steady employment, the pay was sufficiently generous to compensate for the layoffs. At first, when work assignments caused long absences from home, our family life seemed disrupted. But, in time, an unanticipated, salutary strengthening of my parent's marriage resulted. After many weeks separation, those periodic joyful reunions refueled their passions and reinforced their mutual commitment. So the marriage survived, and I had a comfortable, almost middle-class, upbringing.

"It's hard to describe my singular mother. She was remarkably independent, personally quite private, yet generous and thoughtful of others. Though always very loving and caring to us, she did come across as tough, ramrod straight, and highly opinionated—so different from my shitaa's reserved, quiet, non-confrontational demeanor. When I got old enough to meaningfully notice my parent's interactions, it became obvious that she dominated my father. He always agreed with her, and never to my knowledge, became angry or raised his voice. I think her decision to marry him was viewed as a gift, for which he remained forever grateful. The one issue about which she was unyielding, was the demand—not request—that no alcoholic beverages would be allowed in the house. Furthermore, she often repeatedly warned my father, that if he ever came home drunk, she would pack up and leave. He wasn't a teetotaler, or a real drinker, so he never challenged her threat. I had no doubts that she meant what she said.

"For the longest while, I couldn't understand her rigid attitude about alcohol, considering how popular it was with most people. As though reading my mind, one day she surprised me with an astonishing story of her youth, while my father was gone on a job. For the first time, unsolicited, she had opened a window into her childhood, to reveal how alcohol abuse had traumatized and almost destroyed her life.

"My younger sister had been put to bed and the two of us were sitting in the living room. I was reading a school book and mother had a newspaper. It was a cold, blustery night, with fall leaves piling up outside as an early harbinger of winter. We had our first fire of the season that evening, which pleasantly replaced the chilled air as it warmed the room. Also, the fire's bewitching, flickering flames and crackling sound—as moisture exploded from the newly cut logs—were relaxing and soothing.

"I suspect fire's appeal to humans originated aeons past—in the earliest of ancient days—when man first discovered how to control fire. The incredible improvement in life and safety that resulted is hard for us to appreciate. This mastery doubtlessly could be considered the critical revolutionary salient moment in human history, which made possible our species dominance. The mastery of fire gave man untold advantages. We not only survived but thrived, and soon gained an unchallenged ascendancy over all other creatures. It seems the memories of those awesome events from the dawn of history were programmed into our DNA, so when looking into a fire we still evoke a contemplative mood, as did our ancestors.

"Well, I have strayed too far. So, genug, back to that fateful night.

"My relaxed mood was interrupted when I noted how strangely different my mother looked, as she stared into the fire. Then without any preamble she started to talk, and what I heard profoundly changed my life.

"In a strained, yet quiet voice—that even as a child I recognized was burdened with both pride and bitterness—she calmly said,

'Daryl, it's all about those damned Scotch/Irish genes. We're a stubborn bunch, who've spread adventurously all over the bloody world, but have dragged along with us a fatal alcoholic addiction, like some crazy aunt. I know all about alcohol's grim destructive impact from painful experience. My earliest recollections are of my family's continuous struggle for basic survival in some god-awful Pennsylvania coal mining village. And if that weren't enough, we were also regularly brutalized by an alcoholic father.'

"She paused, took a deep breath, and continued.

'During the week, he managed to stagger to work down into the mines, while only half sober. Nobody paid any attention, since most of the men were in the same condition. But on the weekends he was committed to a drunken binge. If he had his feckless way, all his pay would have gone to buy booze. We would have starved were it not for my mother's weekly courageous confrontations with him at the paymaster's desk, where she physically grabbed as much money as possible. She wasn't the only wife battling the bottle, so the company turned a blind eye, and didn't interfere.'

"She paused again as a sob escaped. Her head momentarily tipped down. After a bit, she seemed composed, looked up and resumed. But the depth of her emotional turmoil gave her voice an odd throaty sound.

'We all dreaded my father's angry intoxicated late night returns. When he eventually staggered home, barely able to stand upright, his nauseating smelling breath, besoiled clothes, and booming profane language fouled our lives. As children we were sickened and terrorized, but for my helpless mother it meant a pitilessly, brutal beating. I vowed as a child, and reaffirmed ever since, that if a drunken man raised his hand to me I would immediately leave—or maybe even kill him.' She hesitated, ran her hands through her hair, and mingled with a throb of anguish, said, 'I didn't wait long, and as soon as I could I fled . . . and never looked back.'

"The power and intensity of her story stunned me," mumbled Daryl through clenched teeth. "Maybe shocked would be a better word. I never imagined such an appalling childhood. I was unable to say a word. She hadn't turned to look at me while she spoke, but kept fixated on the fire, as though watching ghostly images of her painful past conjured in the conflagration. In a way, she was talking to herself. No discussion or explanation followed.

She shook her head as though to dispel the wretched memories, and returned to reading the newspaper. She never raised the subject again. As a youngster, I was too overwhelmed and intimidated, even embarrassed, to ask questions. Now as an adult, I realize that in telling her story all those conflicts and troubling recollections had resurfaced, old emotional torments and fears had returned, with an unsettling impact. I can testify to how shattering such old memories can be. And so can you for that matter.

"I further suspect that, despite the justification and courage it took in leaving home, she likely harbored guilt for abandoning her mother and siblings. Worries about their welfare, and uncertain survival, could still haunt her. As far as I know, she never contacted them again.

"When we reached school age, mother (I never thought to call her mother in Apache) decided to get a job. She was still quite young, and very attractive. Her lustrous reddish-brown hair and pale white skin with a scattering of freckles were in vivid contrast to my father's black hair and blemish-free, light-tan coloring. They were a striking couple. Years later, I was surprised to learn that she worked as a librarian. When I questioned her, she was delighted to talk about her career at length.

'Even though I lacked formal education, here's where those awesome Scotch/Irish genes paid off big. They imbued me with a love of books, stories of all sorts, and of course music—which I realized were an inherent, and preciously visceral part of me. Furthermore, I always believed there was something magical about the printed word. Books expanded my knowledge of the world's different peoples who lived in wondrous places with fascinating lives, and books also stimulated my mind with new and challenging ideas. Without leaving home, I could select to be transported out of myself to wherever I chose, or even read about scientific discoveries, while my favorites were the great explorers. By the way, I never understood folks who told me they didn't read books. I truly pity them.'

"Her pride in her career was obvious from her remarks," added Daryl, then continued:

'It didn't take the head librarian long to recognize my talents,' mother smilingly boasted, 'especially when I helped folks find books, and even suggested titles and authors. People welcomed my assistance, and soon many sought me out. I think my days working in the library were my happiest ever. Of course the pay wasn't much at first, but as time went on, and my responsibilities increased, the income improved commensurably.'

"Say, Izak, this is supposed to be an Apache story, yet here I am talking at length about my mother."

"Daryl, let me tell you how mesmerized I am by your story. It's tahkeh ("certainly") a heartwarming tale, which is an important part of who you are. Ich bet eich ("I beg you") continue," urged the Rabbi.

"Well, I certainly didn't get my literary and writing talents, such as they are, from my Apache father. He was a good guy, but clearly not an intellectual. It seems some of those Scotch/Irish genes—hopefully the good ones are dominant—were passed on to me, even though I physically resemble my father. Such goes the inherited chromosomal scramble of characteristics and talents. Reproduction is like a crapshoot— the new resulting mix is unpredictable. My sister, on the other hand, looked like my mother, but lacked her literary interest.

"Now let me reach back to the Apache influences in my life. The Apache part

was considerably vague and hard to identify with, except through my grandfather,
with whom I did spend a lot of time as a
child. We all lived in the same town, some
place in Oklahoma. When my father left
for work out in the oil fields, and could be
gone for many weeks, my mother often
took us to my grandfather's. He lived
alone, not far away in a nice rancher,
which I remember being impressed with
how neat and well cared for it always
looked. I never knew my grandmother.
My mother told me she died from her
first pregnancy, and barely lived long
enough to deliver my father. Grandfather
never remarried. Whatever my Apache
heritage I got it from my grandfather. Naturally, I always called him my 'shickoo'
("grandfather in Apache"). He was glad to
have us (my younger sister and I) stay with
him while mother went to work, and his
sincere affection for us was obvious. We
thrived on his devoted attention, and eagerly looked forward to visits. While there
he made sure we never missed a day of
school, which shickoo repeatedly reminded us was very important and encouraged
our very best efforts.

"Izak, I must credit our dialogues with
stimulating my interest in the Apaches. In
addition to the few tales my shickoo liked

to tell, I did some research. I must say how impressive are the volumes of available information about the Apaches, but also how overwhelmed I am with my remarkable ancient people.

"In brief, their story is mixed—heroic exploits, fierce resistance to pressures to limit their freedom and way of life, and the final pathos of their disintegration.

"For longer than anyone knows, these independent people lived off the land as hunters and gatherers, with the buffalo as the main source for food, tepees, clothing and tools. Ranging widely across the central plains throughout the Southwest into the mountains, they supplemented their diet with wild plants such as the fruit of the cactus. I have learned that the name Apache translates into 'fighting men,' which by all accounts reflects on their fierce warrior culture. Curiously, unlike other Native tribes, they considered fish, dogs, snakes, and turkeys as unclean and wouldn't eat them. They were true nomads, and were linguistically linked to several diverse tribes. I was surprised to learn of the highly respected and central role of women in tribal life. Furthermore, their notable symbol of the circle as the representation of the continuous circle of life from birth to death, though deceptively simple on the surface, was conceptually profound. The Apaches extended their wanderings down into the lands just north of what is now Mexico, where they encountered the Spanish explorations under the command of Coronado, in the mid-1500s. This unexpected confrontation permanently changed the life of the Apaches for the better—they saw horses for the first time; realized their immense value; and used all their energies and guile to acquire them. With stealth and bravery, they stole many horses from the Spaniards, and caught those grazing freely. It didn't take the Apaches long to learn how to ride, train, and breed them. For a while, no one was a match for the mounted Apaches, who quickly expanded their territorial control, dominated the high plains, and terrorized many tribes.

"History's eventual unfolding brought an abrupt end not only to the Apache hegemony, but also to the myriad ancient Indian tribal cultures across the continent. The ever-westward surge of European settlers, backed by Federal cavalry, were unstoppable. Tragically, the resulting disintegration of the Native American civilizations, including the Apache's, were abetted and hastened by the ravages of European diseases, such as small pox, chicken pox, and measles, to which they had no immunity. These almost genocidal epidemics, so weakened and demoralized the Native survivors, that they were unable to sufficiently recover to sustain an effective resistance against the 'invaders.'

"The glory of the widely diverse Native civilizations that had spread across this land ended fairly abruptly by the late 1800s. They were vastly outnumbered by the newcomers, and certainly no match for the European technology. Unfortunately, the white men also lacked appreciation for the richness of these Indian cultures, which contributed to the systematic killing of Natives when they resisted. Progressively the Native lands were taken, and their civilizations wantonly destroyed, without even a modicum of compassion. Typically, the Indians were viewed as subhuman, uncivilized infidels, which validated barbarous acts necessary to subdue and destroy them. In balance, this era was a sad and disgraceful chapter in American history."

The Rabbi who had been listening intently then sighed, nodded, and mumbled, "Amen."

Chapter Six

"I think I'm really getting old," mused Izak Asher as he sat in the lounge waiting for Daryl. His chuckle to himself was loud enough for others in the room to turn with startled looks. With a smile he waved that all was well. Continuing his reverie, Izak nodded and admonished himself for such a shlechte ("wrong") idea. "There're no doubts. Of course I'm getting older, vos zogt ich ("what am I saying"). No one ever gets younger, Got tsu danken ("thank God"). Though the old body is showing considerable wear and tear, I should be grateful that my mind seems to still operate reasonably well; particularly my memory hasn't failed yet. Now, why did I get so shmulky ("sad") today? My spirits are usually lifted when I expect Daryl. Maybe it's the cloudy, unseasonably cool weather, perhaps with a drop in the atmospheric pressure. I've been authoritatively told by Mr 'know-it-all' Gotlieb that the pressure drops cause emotional depression. Maybe he's right. More likely it's my aging biochemistry, whatever that means. Oi vai iz mir ("woe is me"). Genug mit this kind of thinking. Let's see. Do I have a story for Daryl? I'm really impressed with that boy, how he opened up with his family's story last time. He's coming out of his shell, and will surely be able to live a better life, and—hopefully—avoid the demon alcohol. Ah! Here he is, right on time."

Daryl walked leisurely across the room, nodded and smiled to the other occupants, who in turn smiled back. When he reached the Rabbi he offered his right hand for their usual greeting. Their relationship had matured into a comfortable friendship, and the silent handshake became more than a hurried formality—they firmly held hands, smiled warmly at each other, and deliberately prolonged the contact as if to strengthen and reaffirm their bond. Finally, Daryl quietly said, "Shalom, Izak." And in turn, Izak's "Shalom, Daryl," completed the friendly ritual.

"So, Daryl," asked the Rabbi, "what have you been up to? Also I'm glad to see you look so much better, and your clean-shaven face helps. Maybe you've got a new girl friend? That always works. I know how such things can give energy and joy to one's life. Believe me, I wasn't always a dried up old man. Among the blessings of life, our ability to love and embrace another is truly the most magnificent of our human capacities and needs. I hope if love hasn't come your way as yet that it will soon. Ah. Here I am rambling along while you're still standing. Please forgive my rudeness, and zets zikh ahveck ("sit down")."

"Well, about girl friends," Daryl replied, "I must grant that until recent days I haven't been too involved. But, admittedly, back in college," he added with a grin, "I had a very active social life, often to the neglect of my studies. I remember falling in-and-out of love on a regular basis. Also, as a first-string running back on the football team I became a bit of a campus hero, especially among the coeds. Moreover, my exotic Indian appearance, with dark hair braided into a long ponytail, sure appealed to some gals."

As Daryl's smile faded, it was replaced with a grim expression. He turned away and his head tipped down. The Rabbi leaned forward to hear what he said. "But when I first returned from Nam, I had difficulty finding a stable footing, and slipped deeper into alcohol—which started over there as a crutch for dulling my senses so I could function despite near-crippling emotional strains. Somehow, the drinking eventually had an opposite effect: the more I drank the worse I felt. My anxiety and fear intensified to where I hardly slept. By the time I returned to the States, I was a wreck. I'm embarrassed at how long I pathetically floundered, and, under the circumstances, I couldn't sustain any meaningful relationships, particularly with women."

After a lengthy pause, which the Rabbi chose not to interrupt, Daryl straightened up, looked at the Rabbi once again, and in a strong confident voice said, "I'm much relieved, very pleased with myself, and can state how all that's changed. I haven't had a drink in many weeks. Once I admitted that I'm a drunk, and that alcohol was to blame for my weakened resolve while also destroying my health, I knew I was going to lick it. I'd like to confess. I'm cold sober, feel physically strong and energetic, and have a clear head. Genug about all that, eh." Daryl couldn't help smile at his use of Yiddish as he continued. "The new me has finally been able to relate to people—translate that into women— and in the spirit of telling all, I have been seeing someone I met at the paper."

The Rabbi didn't say anything for a while, giving Daryl ample time to marshal his thoughts. Finally the Rabbi said, "Mazel tov ("congratulations") for giving up alcohol, and may you continue to have the strength in your resolve never to use it again. So, look at you. Already with a lady friend. I rejoice with you, and extend my hopes for continued happiness. Life for the new Daryl is just beginning. The possibilities are limited only by your imagination and determination. I predict that someday I'll tell people that I knew the famous journalist-author when he just started. Of course, I'll boast how right off I recognized the talent, when I looked into his eyes." The Rabbi broadly smiled, chuckled, and added, "Just wait and see."

The interaction of these two men—who were so totally unalike in all respects—surprised and pleased both of them. Their freedom and honesty with each other fulfilled fundamental—though differing—needs. Without analysis, it worked and the relationship deepened.

"Now, Daryl," continued the Rabbi, "I must say that your college experience sounds like a typical hundred percent American story—you went to college, not necessarily for the scholastic opportunities but, maybe, as they say, 'to sow your wild oats.' Now don't get me wrong. I don't mean to be critical. I just can't help but view permitting young people such an indulgence as unnecessarily extravagant. If one is not interested in studying, then they have no business in college. Maybe a few years of work out in the real world after high school would help to refocus the motivation. Genug for my unsolicited opinions. Time to bring up important stuff. Tell me . . . how'd you get to be a soldier?"

Daryl smiled at the criticism, which for the most part he agreed with. *Yes,* he thought to himself, the Rabbi is right. *I'll move on to the bloody army stuff.*

"It was my luck to be drafted right after I graduated from college. At the time I didn't have any serious plans, so I reported for induction with a sense of relief that at least for a while I could avoid worrying about what to do with myself. Besides, it all seemed exciting. When I showed up at home in an army uniform, my parents surprised me with totally different reactions. It was an emotional encounter. From my shitaa I received approval and delight. He glowed with pride, tapped me on the back, and quietly said, 'Wait till I tell the guys at the well.'

"Mother, on the other hand, was very upset. One look at the uniform, and before I knew it she had thrown her arms around me, hugged me tightly, and cried uncontrollably. It was the first time I ever saw her openly cry, and I couldn't remember the last time she embraced me. I was stunned speechless. Slowly she composed herself, and her comments came harsh and critical. I'll never forget how she pushed back, held me tight by the shoulders, looked up into my eyes, her face streaked with tears, and asked in an unlikely shrill voice, 'Why the hell didn't you run off to Canada like so many other young men? There's no shame in avoiding an unwarranted, unmitigated hellish disaster, created by over-fed grown men in plush offices, for which young men will pay a bloody price. I bet those damned politicians likely fortified themselves with a martini in one hand, as they hatched their perverted macho schemes.'"

Daryl stopped talking and looked drained by his highly charged recollections. Pulling himself together, he soon went on, "At the time I rejected mother's statements as those of an hysterical female. But after just barely surviving the nightmarish war in Vietnam—with its appalling chaos, unbelievably enormous waste of human lives, both killed and cruelly injured—I came to recognize that my mother was incredibly wise and remarkably prophetic."

Neither man spoke for a while. Daryl appeared unsettled and lost in his own painful thoughts. The Rabbi hesitated to offer comforting words, believing it was best for Daryl to come to grips with the past on his own. Speculating to himself, the Rabbi concluded that though Daryl's talk had reopened some deeply emotional wounds—and likely for the first time—the experience should help.

Finally, Daryl looked up, managed to nod and say, "Izak, forgive my unloading such difficult tales on you. But I do feel better. You're right. Talking about upsetting memories helps make them more tolerable.

"Now I want to bring up something different. Since I saw you last, I did some research—more like an investigation—and I visited two Synagogues. One was very Orthodox, and the other a modern Reformed congregation. What a difference! Hard to believe they were both Jewish. Even the buildings looked different. The Reformed was sort of like a contemporary Christian prayer meeting: the service was almost all in English. In contrast the Orthodox service sounded entirely in Hebrew. During a pause in the prayers, one member confirmed my guess that they were reciting and singing in Hebrew. Izak, the two Synagogues were so unalike. I need your help to understand."

"So, you've become an investigative reporter. Good for you. Your horizons are expanding. Zol zein mit glik ("good luck") with your burgeoning career," said the Rabbi with obvious approval. "Now, the answer to your question isn't simple. You've opened one of those complex Jewish byways. Let's see if I can unravel it in a story."

* * *

So What About a Yarmulke

"The story curiously revolves around a skullcap ("yarmulke in Yiddish, and Kippah in Hebrew") that Jewish men wear in the Synagogue. Sounds improbable that a cap could be so important, eh? So, wait and see. Of course the practice is very old. Long ago, as the custom of head-covering became widespread, it eventually attained the equivalent status of 'Law,' and we now find many Orthodox men wearing a hat of some sort at all times.

"But the historic pressures for change among Jews were mounting. Beginning with the increasing migrations of Jews to

America in the mid to late 1800's, which reached historically peak levels in the early 1900's, commitment to the old Jewish religion faltered—many no longer adhered to Orthodox observances and strictures, along with even an erosion in religious conviction among some.

"Unsurprisingly, a radical modification of Orthodox practice emerged in America, called Reform Judaism. In the scramble to adjust to the new country, many immigrant Jews rejected the Orthodox practices of their youth as not only inconvenient, but also fundamentally irrelevant. For these Jews, the newly-found religious freedom and unlimited secular opportunities offered by America were intoxicating—they were released from the pervasive burdens and restrictions of anti-Semitism, and the constraints of authoritarian Jewish Orthodoxy. The bitter memories of the old world were left behind, and they embraced the new with enthusiasm and hope. The freedoms they now enjoyed made them feel as if refreshingly born again.

"Reform Judaism's much watered-down version of the Orthodox Eurocentric religion had wide appeal, and membership grew rapidly. Undoubtedly its success was due in large measure to

Reform's prudent retention of the foundational scripture of Judaism . . . the Hebrew Bible ("Torah in Hebrew, the Old Testament to non-Jews, and referred to as the Pentateuch in Greek"), as its irreplaceable touchstone. Thus the essential continuity with traditional Judaism was sustained.

"Only for Reform this precious Biblical authority was no longer regarded as the sacred revelation to Moses by God—it was now considered as an inspired historical document. Thus, Reform affirmed it would exercise flexibility in pragmatic interpretation of the Torah—guided by modern scholarship and the circumstantially changing needs of the times. Naturally, from an Orthodox viewpoint, any arbitrary manipulation in the meaning of the 'Divine, God-given Bible' was condemned as blasphemous.

"Fundamentally, Reform didn't split from Judaism, but refashioned its practices and altered its legalistic premise to adjust to the new reality—American Jews increasingly were unable to read the Hebrew religious texts, and had for the most part abandoned Yiddish, the age-old communal language, in their rush to speak English and assimilate as inconspicuously as possible. After millenniums of harsh anti-Semitic treatment in Europe, Jews instinctively as if genetically programmed endeavored to quickly adopt the look, speech, and behavior of their new land. Generally, it took a young, native-born American generation to eventually replace the old Jewish anxiety with confidence in their identity.

"These radical Reform changes—such as discarding of skullcaps in the Synagogue (which is now called a Temple)—unquestionably helped Judaism weather the challenges of the 19th and 20th centuries, which made possible (continuing to present times) the Jewish identification and affiliation of many Jews, who otherwise might have drifted from the faith. During this same period, the robust growth of widely differing Jewish congregations here in America gave Jews the welcome opportunity to join a group whose practices met their needs. Like the Christian diversity of Protestant denominations which provided individuals with doctrinal alternatives, so now Jews also had choices of their own. These bold changes in the path to Jewish worship enabled American Judaism to more than survive, but to flourish. The diversity within American Judaism was an historically novel development, which contrary to its naysayers, has proven to be a significant strength.

"Looking back at America in the 1930's, many Jews grew up in essentially secular families. The emphasis was on the possibilities for the future, downgrading their religious heritage. As a matter of course, the yarmulke was summarily rejected, as a vestige of the foreign, mystical, superstitious, ultra-Orthodox irrational beliefs of the old world. The rebuff of Orthodox Judaism targeted getting rid of the little skullcap. Traditional Judaism became foreign and unacceptable to large numbers of Jews.

"On reflection, in Reform's rush to modernize Judaism, more was initially lost than realized. Caught up in the effort, it seems reformers were often overly eager to discard the old, while not recognizing how little of Jewish spirituality remained.

"The personal experience of one middle-aged, successful physician, I'll call Norman, will illustrate my point. For him, Reform Judaism's blandness, minimally ritualistic, uncluttered with a yarmulke, and rejection of the old dietary rules, along with replacement of most Hebrew with English, provided an acceptable Jewish link. Thus identity and membership seemed enough. Or so he thought.

"Like a clap of thunder heralds an approaching storm with sudden change in the weather, the death of Norman's father provoked an unsettling sense of self-awareness. Over and above his grief, he realized that he didn't know how to mourn. He was saddened, but felt a need to somehow perform some act of respect to honor his father's memory.

"Why this issue suddenly emerged is intriguing, yet clearly too complex to needlessly explore. But it is fair to say that Norman had constrained emotions. Undoubtedly, his professional discipline of ministering with calm reassurance to sick and fearful patients had become deeply ingrained. He was troubled at his inability to express a sense of loss. By all measures he was a successful American adult, but was illiterate and poorly prepared to deal with personal life cycle trials. He had deprived himself of the age-old rituals and religious symbols that could help. In his moment of need . . . he turned back to his Synagogue.

"After a while, Norman experienced a revelatory change in understanding. The repetitive prayers to an unseen—whose existence he always found perplexingly suspect—now when intoned in Hebrew took on new meaning. Something mystically unexpected happened when he worshiped in the ancient language of his people—it was as though his voice had joined the echoes of untold prior generations. Its sounds and rhythms stirred him deeply, overshadowing questions of spiritual conviction. What mattered were his connections to the faith and its people. Any personal qualms were put aside for future conjecture.

"Norman felt his Jewish identity more profoundly than ever before. But along with this fulfillment came unexpected emotional burdens—his anguish and bitterness over his people's historic mistreatments increased, as though an old wound had suddenly reopened. At the same time his pride increased in their past and ongoing laudable accomplishments, which also enhanced his self-esteem. He had opened new passionately enriching doors.

"With an expanded sense of self, he recognized more fully than ever before that he was more than a native-born English speaking American, but was also a Jew, firmly linked to his historic people and religion.

Curiously, like his forebears, he now grasped their meaning when they were said to lament, 'we felt like sojourners in strange lands.' Yet in ways he never imagined possible, he felt more grounded in himself than ever before.

"Also, the paraphernalia of Jewish worship—the yarmulke in particular, along with the prayer shawl—took on new meaning. The once strange and foreign ritual of wrapping one's self in them, had become a comforting and profound symbolic act— a tangible and visible affirmation of his essential Jewishness. The little yarmulke was finally restored to its appropriate place of prominence.

"In time, American Reform Judaism has continued to build on its dynamic flexibilty, wherein much of the Jewish tradition has been restored to Synagogue service. So, Daryl, the differences you observed have diminished, and their vital coalescence has increased."

Chapter Seven

The wind had picked up as Daryl walked to the park. *Just look at how fast those puffy white clouds are moving,* he thought. *I'm glad I put on my old army jacket. This time of year the weather's so variable it's hard to know how to dress. Even the paper's predictions are more a suggestion than anything else. I remember how Mr. Lindsohm tried to tell me about the weather.* Daryl chuckled to himself, recalling the explanations about fronts. *The only front I knew at the time was out there in the bush. It wasn't actually a front, like in the days of regular wars, but the general direction where 'Charlie' could be moving around—a real fluid sort of front. The dangerous thing was you never knew what you'd find. Areas recently cleared out and declared 'secure,' could now be swarming with those guys. Enough of that Nam shit.*

Where was I? Oh yeah, I was thinking about the weather, mused Daryl while purposefully ambling along. *Hope the Rabbi dressed warm enough—that is if he made it to the park. No sweat if he didn't, then I'll just walk over to the Home. Now lets see, what can I remember about weather fronts? I think some of it's coming back. They are masses of air, and are called either cold or warm. Old Lindsohm particularly worried about cold fronts. He liked to be ready for them since they could bring fierce thunderstorms with lots of rain, or snow, moisture of some kind, strong winds, and a drop in the barometric pressure with cooler temperatures. Of course he needed rain, but not too much he said, since floods could ruin his crops. Incredible how he had a knack of knowing when a cold front was coming by the direction of the winds. I finally nailed that one down—cold fronts always spin counterclockwise. On the other hand, a warm front is just the opposite—it spins clockwise, barometric readings rise along with the temperature, bringing in nice weather, and occasionally light rain. What confused me at first was to learn that these huge masses of air also moved horizontally— from west to east across the U.S. Amazing I remember any of that stuff.*

Good. There's the Rabbi sitting on his regular bench. I wonder whether I'll be like him when I get old—life filled with repetitive routines. Which reminds me of something I read about change. They found that people react poorly to change. Surprisingly, the study claimed that changes, good or bad, equally tend to shorten life. Who would have thought. If they're right, it's a little unsettling. Seems we humans are less flexible or adaptable than we thought—those few best able to cope with new circumstances survive and could pass on those traits, while the rest who are less resilient succumb early. Listen to me. Here I am sounding like a damned Darwinian. Enough of this stuff. As a final thought, it's sure obvious that folks are comforted by familiar things, surroundings, and specifically people they know.

Glad to see the Rabbi's dressed properly with a heavy coat, gloves and, look at that, a knit hat. First time I saw him wearing one. It also covers his ears, a sensitive place when a cold wind is blowing. Maybe I'll buy one for myself. They say the head's very vulnerable to cold, and when left uncovered quickly loses a lot of body heat. Yep. Best to wear a hat when the temperature drops. Ha! Should I dig up an old army helmet? Stupid thought. Forget the fuckin' war, and focus on the here and now . . . Look at that old guy. Reading the newspaper as usual. There's a lesson here. Keeping yourself interested in

*what's going on in the world must stimu-
late the mind to remain active and healthy.
I wonder whether he reads his Bible any-
more? He's a good example, with a mind
that's sharp as a tack, despite all those
years he piled up. And when I recall the
unthinkable experiences he's lived
through, I wonder how he managed to
remain sane. Yet there's no doubt, the
Rabbi's much better adjusted than I am.*

The Rabbi didn't notice Daryl's approach until he stood in front of him.
When he looked up over the paper, a
broad smile illumined his face and his
eyes glowed with delight. If someone was
watching from afar, they might wonder
about the silence. Neither man spoke for
a while. What couldn't be seen from a
distance were the warm welcoming looks
they exchanged. Finally, the Rabbi nodded and patted the seat next to him, urging Daryl to sit.

"So, Mister Journalist," said the Rabbi
with teasing formality, along with a spar-
kling grin, "what's new? I bet you're surprised to see me out in this blustery
weather. Let me tell you. When the body
gets old and cranky, I find the cold sort of
stirs up the sluggish system, and before I
know it I feel more alive. Of course if I

were to carry this too far, to an extreme, I either burn myself out, or freeze to death." The Rabbi laughed to himself— pleased with his comments— then asked, "How about you, boitshick, do you like the cold?"

"You know me, Izak. I take it as it comes. Maybe if I had to make a choice, I'd say cold." After a brief hesitation, he frowned and concluded, "Could be that hot weather reminds me of those cursed days in Vietnam."

"Ich farshtay. Yeder mentsh hot zein peckel ("I understand. Every man has his burden.")," spoke the Rabbi in uncon- strained Yiddish—the instinctive choice of an old aphorism. But, observing how grim Daryl's expression had suddenly become, the Rabbi hastened to change the subject.

"Now, Daryl, if I'm not mistaken, you still have some good stories waiting to be told. Why don't you take over today? I already had my regular breakfast with a nice crispy bagel— just the way I like them—the walk out here warmed me up. I read the paper, but with no disrespect meant, it was filled with crime and vio- lence, had nothing redeeming. So I'm ready to listen, and of course be enriched by your tale. They're always filled with such extraordinary chochmeh ("wisdom")."

Daryl smiled, shook his head, paused while thinking to himself, *am I ready to share my farm experience with him, and not leave anything out? Oh, hell, why not!*

"Izak, you have encouraged me to talk about an unusual experience. I hope you're receptive to hear about rather personal intimacies."

"Daryl, don't hold back. There's nothing in human behavior, whether sublime or depraved, that could shock me. Regrettably, I've had to accept that it's all part of our mutual potentials."

* * *

Farmer Lindsohm

"Chip Nelson, one of the guys from Nam, suggested that after living through all that shit, what I needed was to work on a dairy farm for a while. Forever joking, his subtle pun took a while for me to get it. When I did, we both laughed hysterically. It wasn't really that funny, but our outsized reaction only expressed how emotionally strung-out we were.

"He figured shoveling real cow shit for a change would be like a great rehab. Since he was a farm boy from Wisconsin he knew what he was talking about. Of course at the time I couldn't imagine working on a farm, so took his home phone number and politely promise to call.

"Not to dwell on the prolonged drunken holiday I indulged in when I got back to the States, it suffices to say I eventually sobered up enough to realize I was going nowhere. Though my alcohol saturated brain was clouded and fuzzy, I by chance recalled Chip's suggestion. In desperation I called him, and what enfolded turned out better than I expected, and might have saved my life.

"Chip was a real pal. No questions were asked. He came through without hesitation, and even sounded glad to hear from me. Before I could change my mind, he had arranged a job. Through his contacts he found what he felt was a perfect place for me—it was on a small farm owned by Johan Lindsohm, out in the middle of the dairy lands of Wisconsin. Chip's proud accounts of his family's farm, and how he planned to return there and never leave, had filled many of our otherwise restless, dreary nights. I can't remember how often he boasted about how Wisconsin was the leading producer of milk, cheese, and butter in the country.

Though I only half listened to his enthusiastic droning, it was a helpful distraction—I relaxed mentally, and my chronically knotted muscles loosened a bit as I stretched out. At the time I didn't care about anything. If asked my opinion in those days I always replied, 'I don't give a shit.' I also must confess, that I even entertained the awful thought that if I were killed then my suffering would gratefully end."

The Rabbi was upset by Daryl's words, but restrained his impulse to offer a response. In an attempt to hide his distress he silently looked down and knowingly only nodded—as if to say, 'I understand. I've been there.'

"While traveling on a bus from the Dane County Regional Airport, in Madison, Wisconsin, heading upstate to the city of Portage, Chip's stories came back. Just like he had described—I saw wide open expansive agricultural fields, punctuated by freshly painted farmsteads and outbuildings, with their obelisk-like silos ubiquitously decorating the landscape. As the bus traveled straightaway along a snowplowed blacktop road, I was literally dazzled by what I saw stretching to the horizon. It all seemed unreal and overwhelming. My unhealthy transition to civilian life had left me deeply troubled psychologically with a persistent feeling of unhealthiness, which clouded my perception and constrained my emotions. The alcoholic binges had heightened my tensions, general anxiety, and fatigue. My mind suddenly wandered in a perverse direction—I longed for the army discipline where I didn't have to think, but was told what to do . . . and worst of all, I even missed those terrifying patrols. Don't get me wrong, Izak, not the patrols themselves. It was for the incredibly intense euphoria that I craved, which always followed my uninjured return to our base, miraculously having survived once again. Like an addict, I hungered for those magnificent highs, and relished them as a well-earned reward. Regularly after a patrol, following the caring for the wounded and the dead, the rest of us always wildly celebrated with abandon, consuming vast amounts of booze and or drugs, which were somehow readily available, while incessantly smoking weed. Our highs and lows could likely be described as certifiably manic. At the time I brooded with a private macabre foreboding—if the Vietcong stormed us during a bacchanal indulgence when we were so entirely wasted as to be unable to defend ourselves, we would certainly all be killed. Fortunately, they never attacked during those vulnerable lapses. Maybe like us, after a bloody battle, Charley also over-indulged and got zonked out.

"Some people seemed to easily reestablish themselves in civilian life. But I didn't. On reflection, my life was so sadly bereft of meaningful purpose that I was incapable of imagining a productive path forward. Also, I now realize that when I persistently leaned heavily on an alcoholic crutch, it was a futile, escapist, self-destructive choice; a bad choice which only made things worse.

"As the bus moved along, I couldn't take my eyes off the farms. I wondered whether I would make it out here. Though my hunger for peace and tranquility burned fiercely in my tormented consciousness, I feared the effort was beyond my reach.

"Lindsohm finally arrived at the Portage bus stop to pick me up as planned, in a stunning, large new model Cadillac. After the long tedious bus ride, I chose to stand outside of the little station building despite the cold wintry weather. Though it wasn't snowing at the time, the sky was covered with a curtain of low hanging dark gray clouds, ominously threatening to momentarily add to the already heavy snow cover. The gloomy day didn't help to lighten my already melancholy mood, likely affected by the mental and physical let-down as my blood alcohol level dropped. True to form, I had hidden a quart of vodka in my duffle bag as a back-up, while promising myself—not for the first time—that I would stop drinking and dry out.

"I rapidly walked back and forth during my restless wait, becoming increasingly anxious and wondering whether this was all a mistake. When the sedan finally pulled up I was relieved that I hadn't been forgotten, and admittedly quite awed by the expensive automobile. I never imag-ined the farming business paid so well. Lindsohm got out on the passenger side—the possible significance of which didn't register with me at the time—slowly strolled over, looked at me for an extend-ed moment, and then said, 'I'm Johan Lindsohm. Can I assume you're Daryl?' I answered in the affirmative. He stuck out a large, calloused hand in greeting, while a friendly grin failed to mask the sad, con-cerned look in his eyes, and slowly added, 'Well, son, you've come a long way so let's not delay getting you settled.'

"The trip probably took longer than usual since we slowed down when it began snowing and the windshield wipers worked hard to clear the view. As the car pulled up the long, moderately inclined driveway to the farm I heard the tires spinning through the snow, searching for a grip on the frozen underlying gravel surface. The high pitched sound put my taut nerves on edge. During the drive from the bus stop to the farm, I was puzzled at the lack of conversation. Fatigue and disorientation inhibited any comments of my own, so I hunkered down in the back seat, lost in somber musings.

"When Lindsohm got out of the car, I was surprised that the driver stayed put with the motor idling. Before closing the car door, Lindsohm leaned in and said, 'Thanks, Peter.' The car then made a u-turn in the yard and left. Now I was even more confused. Lindsohm apparently noticed my perplexed expression, turned and said in his easy, quiet manner, 'My neighbor, Peter, was good enough to give me a lift while my truck was in for repairs.' The shock of his comment hit me like a blast of cold water. Any fanciful assumptions I had about Lindsohm's wealth were shattered, and disappointment deepened my depression. Furthermore, as I looked around, the peeling paint on the adjacent barn and on the old farmhouse—just visible through the heavy snow flakes and the fading daylight— were signs of neglect. Not what I had envisioned.

"I stood still, as if waiting for instructions, and concluded that some Wisconsin farmers might be prosperous, but Farmer Lindsohm surely didn't look like one of them.

"My memory of that first evening remains blurred. It's not as though something terrible happened. On the contrary, everyone did their best to welcome me, but the strangeness was almost more than I could handle. My old battle-conditioned reaction of mental withdrawal from a threatening situation took over. I looked down, nibbled on the food, and was grateful when the meal ended that my weird behavior hadn't been too embarrassing.

"I do clearly remember sitting on the bed in my attic room that night, debating with myself whether I should keep my clothes on when I got into bed since the room was as cold as a refrigerator, while sipping from the bottle of vodka. I didn't need to justify that small drink by blaming the day's strain and difficulty, since drinking was a routine habit—part of my life. Strangely, I hadn't recognized I was a drunkard. While holding the bottle at arm's length, I vowed out loud to kick the habit now that I'd settled down—as I pitifully took a final gulp.

"The last thing Lindsohm said when he wished me a good night's rest, was to remind me of his 4:30 morning wake-up call. I remember the time, since I asked him to repeat it. Despite the discordant circumstances, I slept well. Johan—which he insisted I call him—right on schedule called from the bottom of the steps, 'Good morning, Daryl. Time to get up.' He repeated the call until I answered. This was the beginning of many new and difficult experiences, yet invigorating and restorative.

"To put it simply, my adjustments to the routines and chores of working a dairy farm were incredibly abrupt. From that first day, it was like learning to swim by jumping into the water and figuring it out. There weren't any preparatory talks; I was expected to learn on the run; perform assigned tasks; and without much discussion, or supervision for that matter, get the job done. With Johan busy with the milking, and short on small talk, I was increasingly working alone. After an exhausting first day, by early evening I looked forward to my cold room and bed.

"That first morning sticks in my memory. The prior day's snowstorm had ended sometime in the night, and I was surprised how quickly the weather had changed for the better. It was dark as we left for the barn, and the silence in the house indicated that the rest of the family was still asleep. There was something eerie, yet stimulating, how Johan and I were the only two people moving out into a frigid, empty, darkened landscape. The starless night sky was crystal clear with nary a cloud in sight, and the stunning illumination from a full moon reflected off the ground's enveloping blanket of un-trampled white snow, barely turning night to day. I followed along to the barn, crunching through the frosty snow, while exhaling misty vapors in the sub-freezing air, noting that no lights could be seen off in the distance from other farms. It looked like we were the eager early risers.

"Without delay, and in an offhand fashion, I learned the basics: chores each morning preceded breakfast; and the world of dairy farming was governed unalterably by the need to milk the cows seven days a week—never on any erratic or varying schedule, but on a rigidly fixed timetable of twice a day. Moreover, every drop of milk was valued—it was the only 'cash crop.' Not surprisingly, the better the quality of milk, the more Johan was paid. He explained, 'There were three variables which factored into the calculation—volume, butterfat content, and bacteria count.' He would benefit from large volume and high butterfat, but was penalized by high bacteria counts. The commercial dairy, which picked up the large milk cans every morning, kept records of milk production, and along with the monthly payments included an accounting of how each variable impacted on the net income. Johan always carefully scrutinized the statements, and liked to share some findings with me. Especially when the bacteria counts had risen, he would shake his head dolefully and say, 'We had to be more diligent.'

"He often used the expression, 'Running a dairy farm was like a juggling act', and proudly offered how he was a master at balancing the variables to his best advantage. It took some time before he got around to explaining how he controlled the butterfat and volume. But, on the very first day, he seriously talked more about bacteria control than anything else. I watched as he meticulously washed each cow's teats with warm water before connecting the automatic milking machines. The lesson was obvious—cleanliness began with the cow—reducing the bacteria contamination at the main source was critical. So, my job each day was to scrub the backsides of each cow with a stiff bristle brush to remove all traces of dried manure. Not a very edifying procedure. To be fair, I couldn't blame the animals for fouling themselves, since now in winter they spent the days in the barn with their heads confined within a stanchion (a device that loosely fits around a cow's neck and limits forward and backward motion, but allows them to lie down). When they must urinate and void their bowels it is unavoidably deposited where they stand and sit. The cows have no choice in the matter, and likely don't give it any thought. It's the finicky humans who are appalled.

"Talking about cow manure reminds me that I spent much of my time responsible for it, one way or another. Every morning after breakfast, I dug in with my pitchfork and removed the prior day's waste accumulations around each cow. When a wheelbarrow was filled, I emptied it into a manure spreader (a tractor-pulled, big two-wheeled wagon) parked just outside one end of the barn. I then replaced the soiled straw around and under each cow. The straw (the dry stalks of cereal crops after their threshing) was the invaluable bedding for the animals, and absorbed and entrapped the waste, facilitating its containment and collection. Straw is indigestible by humans, but I found it remarkable to learn that since cows can digest it, a small amount is often added to their diet as roughage.

"My first sight of the manure spreader in action caught me by surprise. I hadn't given it any thought, so when Johan announced that the wagon was filled and needed to be spread, I became a little tense. I expected my job would be to stand in the spreader and shovel off the manure as the spreader was dragged across the field by the tractor. An unattractive and tedious prospect. Silently I waited for instructions, only to be told to come outside and watch. I breathed a sigh of relief that my assumption was wrong. When Johan drove into position on a field, the spreader was activated and began to hurl the manure up in the air. The mechanical belt driven device on the spreader's floor moved the manure to the rear where it was broken and scattered by metal beaters). It was a strange sight as the wagon lumbered forward—like raining shit.

But it made sense. Johan was fertilizing his fields. The tractor moved at a slow speed, and left the widely broadcast 'natural' fertilizer in its wake. These brown, irregularly sized and shaped manure particles spread out on the surface of the frozen unblemished white snow, clearly marked a treated field. But in addition, I recognized Johan's method: it was a self-sustaining cyclical system of dairy farming (a standard dairying operation). Conservation governed. I had never encountered such care not to waste anything, even in the military. On the farm, everything seemed to be utilized directly or indirectly.

"That smelly, overabundant manure is where the cycle began. Incidentally, when I first arrived, the odor seemed to permeate everything. I couldn't get away from it, and almost felt sick. But curiously, it didn't take long before I couldn't smell the manure at all. Interesting, eh?

"The manure enriched soil nourished the growth of an abundant crop of field corn (which along with grasses were finely chopped and fermented to produce a rich cow feed called 'silage'); and the manure also fed various grasses, which when harvested and dried became hay (the cow's staple food). Of course, the cow's milk, the quintessential end-product of this well-integrated cycle, not only directly nourished the farmer's family, but also provided for his essential cash income. And to return to the cycle's beginning: as long as the cows were adequately fed, they never failed to generate ample quantities of manure, which in turn sustained the entire process. Beautiful and extraordinary.

"It took a while for Johan and I to get beyond my novice status, and become sufficiently relaxed with each other to explore wider conversations. We had our first real talk one day when we had gone out to his woods on the tractor to cut down a tree. It turned out that the huge, cast-iron kitchen stove burned wood. The amount needed to keep the stove fire going was considerable. This wooded area, on the back end of his property, was not overly extensive, and the number of trees seemed woefully finite. I couldn't help reflect to myself, that when the trees had all been cut down, what then? I figured the forest didn't have long to live.

"Once I demonstrated how handy I was with an ax, Johan was delighted to give me the time-consuming and wearisome job of splitting the cut logs. Moreover, I had to keep an eye on the supply of logs in the kitchen, to make sure we were never caught short.

"Having finished the bottle of vodka, I soon struggled with alcohol withdrawal. The early days were the most difficult—I felt irritable, out of sorts, couldn't shake an overwhelming sadness which weighed me down (doctor's call it depression), along with bouts of nausea, and trouble sleeping. But I never gave up, and despite how lousy I felt, I kept functioning. During this period I credited the long, hard hours of work with helping me get through it. Whenever I felt particularly agitated, I ran out to the woodshed as soon as possible and vigorously split logs. Johan probably recognized that I was going through some illness, or adjustment, the nature of which he didn't know, and never asked, even when I must have looked sick. I didn't explain anything, struggled silently, and felt the battle with alcohol was my private affair. Gratefully the withdrawal symptoms cleared in a few weeks. During that difficult period, all he offered, in his low key, taciturn fashion, was how pleased he was with all the split logs.

"Johan broke the conversational ice that day out in the woods while I was chopping down the tree. With one elbow resting on the tractor, chewing on his unlit pipe, and looking off into the distance, he quietly said, 'Chip told me you and he were buddies out in Vietnam. At first when he approached me about you, I rejected the idea, since I needed help with an experienced hand. But when he talked a bit about what it was like out there: awesome casualties all around; how steady, dependable and helpful you always were; and how miraculously you and he got through alive . . . I reconsidered.'

"I was surprised by his comment, and at first couldn't think of anything to say. Neither of us spoke for a while. He slowly lit his pipe, and I rested the ax head on the ground. At this point I hadn't talked about my war experiences to anyone, and thus hadn't dealt with all the confusing and troubling recollections I tried not to think about. I wasn't ready to do so, nor did I think this was the time to grapple with those issues, but I owed him an honest response.

"We both had turned and were looking at each other. Finally I said, 'Johan, let me thank you for giving me the opportunity to work on your farm. You took a chance, and I hope I haven't been a disappointment.' I paused, gathered myself, and continued, 'What people don't understand, though you might, is that 'Nam was not just a nightmare, it was an unremitting horror.' When I started talking, the words just flowed out of control. I couldn't help adding, 'If at times I appear strange and unfocused, it's when those unbidden memories suddenly awaken with an unsettling reality. I feel like I'm back there again, nearly crippled with fear, immobilized, and desolate for a while.'

"Concerned that maybe I had said too much, I forced myself to stop talking. I also felt excited and nervous. *Perhaps,* I reflected, *had I destroyed Johan's image of me as some sort of macho hero, by revealing myself as an emotional wreck?* Johan's deep sorrowful eyes never lost contact with me, but had somehow refocused with a strange haunting cast.

"His sober expression didn't change as he listened, and in silent acknowledgment he rhythmically nodded up and down. Though his tired eyes remained fixed on me, he looked as though he envisioned some far off disturbing image. He was physically here, but had mentally connected to some appalling place.

"Johan shook his head, squinted a few times, took a couple of puffs on his pipe, and asked so softly that I barely heard,

'Daryl, did you ever get involved with helicopters over there?'

'Ha, what a question,' I hastily answered. 'Those copters were our magic carpets. They flew us deep into the bush, somehow always found a little clearing just barely big enough, and set us down as gently as if we were getting off a commuter plane back home. But, most important, we were confident they would come back to haul our bloody (I mean that literally) asses out of there. Sustained by that knowledge, we did our job and, it goes without saying, our lives ultimately depended on them. They never failed us. Without those copter jockeys none of us would have made it back home.'

"Johan, stood a little straighter, his voice sounded forced and throaty, with a slight stammer, and his eyes misted over when he asked, 'Daryl, did you by chance run into a Huey pilot named Lars?. . . Lars Lindsohm . . . my son?'

"I knew instantly that Lars never made it back. The ax fell from my hand, and before I knew it I had taken Johan in my arms. We both broke down and sobbed loud and uncontrollably. Our deeply buried anguish, fueled with much unexpressed anger, had burst forth, maybe for the first time. Alone out in the woods we were freed from the customary inhibiting tangle of restraints, and like a clap of thunder announcing a violent storm, we surrendered to our emotions. Without the firm grasp of our arms, we might have fallen to the ground.

"One day shortly thereafter, I wasn't surprised when Johan mentioned, 'Cristin is my second wife, and the two youngsters are ours. Lars, and my teenage daughter, Grete, were from the first marriage. Anna had died when Grete was only six, from an aggressive cancer. Cristin is a cousin of Anna, and I needed help, so one thing led to another and we married. She is much younger than I, but is a good woman . . . and we have adjusted.'

"Once the fog of withdrawal lifted, I became a different and better, or should I say normal, person. It had been so long since I was clean, that I couldn't get over the improvement. Life seemed good, I felt vigorous, ate with enthusiasm, liked the world around me, and started to seriously notice Grete for the first time. She left early in the morning for high school, and the only time we leisurely crossed paths was during the evening meal.

"She looked and sounded mature for a 17-year old, and was strikingly beautiful. Her inherited Scandinavian height, her well-rounded figure—clearly both firm and athletic—admittedly was very appealing. But what captivated me was how her lustrous long blond hair loosely framed her face. In addition, her prominent cheek bones and clear light-blue eyes, which contrasted with her soft cream colored unblemished skin, were stunningly alluring. I couldn't help stare at her across the table. Dinner was the only time in the day for the entire family to be together. Though they were a reserved group, with no yelling or talking out of turn, nevertheless, conversation was fairly brisk, but when Grete spoke it sparkled and they all listened. Even Johan stopped eating and looked her way, with an expression of admiration and love, to capture all she said.

"I had little to offer to the family's sharing of the day's experiences, so listened quietly. While not seeming too bold, and trying not to be obvious, I occasionally smiled at Grete. When she smiled back with unambiguous friendliness, my heart raced with delight. It didn't take her long to draw me out when she said, 'Daryl, I notice how well you look, and even the whites of your eyes have lost their blood-shot look. It must be that father's punishing work schedule has done wonders for you. Nothing like Wisconsin's sterile, frozen world to either make or break a man.' And then she added with a chuckle, 'Of course a daily dose of our raw cow's milk is the essential nostrum for good health.'

"I joined in as everyone laughed. What they didn't know was that I couldn't remember the last time I laughed. It felt strange, yet I marveled at how my mood had improved. On reflection, I also realized that Grete had been watching me for some time, and not casually. My heart skipped a beat.

"Little by little Grete and I became some kind of friends. There was never an opportunity to be alone, so we only interacted briefly before, during and after dinner, while folks gathered around the table. Now that I had fully recovered from booze addiction, my previously moribund libido had awakened. Inevitably, she became the central focus of my longings. So once again, I hurled myself feverishly into work to somehow distract and defuse my frustrations. Yet, each evening when we met, and I looked at her smiling face, aglow with energy, all my yearnings returned. I tried to hide my fascination with her from the others, especially from Johan, by doing my best to talk to him, or even to ask Cristin, for instance, whether the wood supply was adequate. My obsession with her had even intruded into my dreams, where lascivious visions of Grete often appeared.

"One night, while reading in bed, as was my practice before going to sleep, I heard my door open. When I looked up, to my astonishment there was Grete standing in the opening, with an incredibly wide smile illuminating her face. I threw the book on the floor, smiled back, and held out my arms. On her way into the room she unbelievably disrobed, slipped under the covers and wrapped herself around me. We didn't speak a word, but hungrily embraced, kissed and made love. I didn't keep count, but we coupled repeatedly. Our need for each other was insatiable. When she finally left, I lay back and wondered was it all a dream. Of course it wasn't. I fell into a deep untroubled sleep, from which Johan had difficulty awakening me with his morning call.

"I had fallen madly in love with Grete, with heedless exuberance. Her periodic visits to my room were all I lived for. Since they were unpredictably spaced, I never knew when she would come, so my ardor was heightened with anticipation. When together, we never seemed to get enough of each other. Finally, after a considerable time, I started to miss some intellectual exchanges with her. Whenever I attempted to talk to her after our bouts of sex, she quickly shook her head with a finger on her lips and pointed downstairs. When I persisted, she put her lips to my ear and whispered, 'My dearest Daryl, we mustn't share our little secret with my parents. My father would be outraged, and probably fire you on the spot.'

"Nonetheless, I still needed to get to know her better. We certainly were compatible in bed, but what else? I was totally seduced, as you can imagine. I think I was addicted once again, but this time to our sexual exploits. With no further effort, I quietly acquiesced to silence, and reveled in my passion. But I couldn't ignore the questions of whether we had any interests in common, and could we plan to live our lives together and not necessarily on a farm?

"Something had to change and it shouldn't have come as a surprise when she whispered one night, 'I missed my period and could be pregnant.' I was stunned, and felt helpless that events were moving faster than I wanted. Was I destined to marry the farmer's daughter, as the old cliché goes? There was no doubt in my mind that I didn't want to spend my life as a dairy farmer. Feeling somewhat trapped, uncertain what to say or do, I succumbed to inertia, and silently muddled along.

"When she came to me at night as usual, a few days after her announcement, I felt something was different. Grete was still eager and loving, but I had changed. Where this was leading preyed on my mind, and I wondered whether the price I would pay was too much. Yet, I savored the physical and emotional comfort I derived from sex with her, and appreciated its immense value—the chronic bodily tension I lived with since 'Nam had vanished, and the cloud of despair and fear through which I viewed the world around me had lifted. My debt to her was enormous. So despite my misgivings, I continued to silently participate, but with a measure of feigned enthusiasm. Since we had never talked, I was unable to truly understand Grete's motivation in initiation of sex. Her actions and behavior were certainly expressions of her own sexual needs, which she had boldly acted on. On the other hand, I liked to think she recognized that I was a troubled war vet, for whom she could provide the most basic pleasure and comfort. But, maybe she had redirected her profound grief for her lost brother, and acted out her accumulated distress with passionate sexual involvement? As a surrogate for her brother, my presence might have awakened mixed emotions, which served to justify her behavior, and even possibly reduced her anguish and calmed her troubled mind.

"Listen to me, Izak, I'm sounding like a shrink. That's what happens when you become a journalist. Before you know it, you're sprouting off like an expert on everything. Now, I'll get back to my story.

"Despite my inner uncertainties, I hungered for her, and was relieved when she finally showed up after a long absence. Her demeanor was different—a mix of joy and sadness. She surprised me by immediately whispering in my ear, 'Daryl, we're not going to be parents. I had an unusually active flow last week, which probably was a miscarriage.' She then almost laughed out loud, quickly clasping a hand over her mouth, and added, 'So. young fella, we'll have to try harder.'

"Before I had a chance to absorb her news, maybe even formulate a reply, she pushed me down, sat on top of me with her legs spread wide, and I had no choice but to respond. Her overactive sexual arousal and demands for repeat performances suddenly dawned on me that she was trying to get pregnant again. At that moment I decided I had to leave the farm.

"Without delay, I approached Johan the following day. I was filled with guilt and regret, and a sense of failure that I was leaving him without a helper. He looked at me with his calm smile and said, 'Daryl, I somehow knew the farming life wasn't for you. Oh, you did splendidly, and I will miss you. What's next?'

"'I think I'll give college a try', I said. 'The G.I. grants, will help. I've often thought that journalism sounded appealing. How about you? Are farmhands available?/'

"'Well, I've heard that some Mexicans have shown up in town. They're a hard working group, so I shouldn't have difficulty finding help.'

Grete obviously heard of my plans to leave and without even a departing smile, literally ignored me. Johan drove me back to the train station, in his truck. He silently handed me an envelope with a check for my work.

We hesitantly shook hands . . . but then he pulled me to him and we hugged. He quietly said, 'Good luck, son. Think of us once in a while, and I would be pleased to get a letter and hear about how you're making out.'

Johan then turned, got into the truck, didn't look back— and left.

Chapter Eight

The Rabbi looked out the window at the neat gently curved white gravel driveway set in a lush green lawn, which led to the front entrance of the Home, and thought: *There is just something a little too sterile about its appearance for my taste. Makes the place look like an institution. Vell, of course it really is, but people live here, and vould be delighted vith scenery that reminded them of a real front yard. So vhy not plant some pretty flowers along vith evergreens and some shrubs to break up the barrenness, and create a haimish ("informal, friendly") feel. Yet, at least they keep the grass mowed and somebody must spend a lot of time vith the gravel. Maybe less vork vith the gravel and more on flowers. After all, this place is called The Home. Making it look more like one makes sense. Listen to me. I'm thinking like some sort of landscape maivin ("expert"). Oh my, I'm such a k'vetsher ("complainer").*

"Now," the Rabbi mumbled, "even the weather looks farshtunken ("stinky"). Those dark clouds have built rapidly, filled the sky, and it will probably storm before long." He shook his head in disappointment, and decided it was best to stay in today.

Within moments a slanting heavy downpour began—driven by a strong wind, mixed with sleet.

"This'll be a depressingly bitter cold day, and I hope Daryl dressed appropriately," he ruefully growled out loud to himself, and turned to head for the lounge.

Suddenly he stopped short. Dreaded, fearful memories had flooded his consciousness: *Oi Vai* ("exclamation of pain"). *Why do I become so moody on a day like this, and then those wretched recollections of the awful past sneak back? Suddenly I feel the painful cold again, as when I had been forced to stand barefooted out in the blowing rain mit the others, dressed in threadbare shirt and pants, and shaking so badly I thought I'd fall. The threatening, heavy-booted guards (most were Germans, although some were Nazis from Eastern Europe) eagerly walked up and down the line, with drawn pistols—a gleam of anticipated delight shown in their eyes—ready to shoot those who fell. Life hung in the balance. Daryl might think I prayed to the Jewish God to hold me up, but he doesn't understand—God had deserted us!*

Ha! That is, if God even existed!

What I did next saved my life: I bit deeply into my lower lip until the blood ran, and hungrily sucked it in. Between the pain and the welcome moisture in my mouth . . . I stayed awake and didn't fall. Genug! Genug!"

For support as he staggered, the Rabbi instinctively grasped the round brass rail that was attached along the walls. The assault of those memories left him weak and depressed. He asked, "Why do those horrors keep coming back? I'm hopeless," he reproached himself. "Can't seem to forget. I must focus on something positive. Well, I did have a good bowel movement this morning. That's an encouraging sign there's still some life left in the old sluggish body."

The Rabbi shook his head, stood upright, and as he resumed his walk to the lounge he happily recalled today was Daryl's visit. The thought brightened his spirits and he muttered to himself, "Daryl has no idea what a blessing his attention has been, and how much I value it. Amazing that our friendship continues to grow. Indeed, my life has been revitalized. I was getting to be a dried-up, faded old coot, lost in bitter memories, and out-of-touch with the world. Now, listen to me, 'old coot.' I'm sounding more and more like a rustic Texan. Nothing wrong with them of course, expect they're nice people. But they're also likely to be uneducated or undereducated, with inflexible beliefs in a wide panoply of superstitions to offset their limited understanding of the puzzling and frightening world. Lives so narrowly circumscribed are often susceptible to the influence of a harsh fundamentalist Christian Church— of which I understand there are many throughout the state. I suspect, if I were to attend services in such a Church, stood up suddenly and boldly announced that I'm a Jew, they'd be shocked with wonder and disbelief . . . at how I somehow stepped out of the Bible."

"I can't get Daryl's story about his time on the farm out of my mind," reflected the Rabbi. "To me, the primary issue that highlighted the tale was his ongoing struggle with alcohol abuse. I admire his determination to break the dependency, and rejoice at his success. To have overcome was immensely laudable, and speaks volumes about the man's strength of character. As a mere   weak and fragile human, like the rest of us, he had a tough job. Moreover, we all inherently need human support and affection. People tend to thrive when they have positive interpersonal experiences. After the trauma of the military (where civilized, humane values were repudiated—of regrettable necessity), Lindsohm's friendly welcome and non-authoritarian quiet manner were just what Daryl needed—a calm, orderly, peaceful, nonthreatening environment.

"But Grete's assertive offering of sexual love unquestionably worked the magic of filling his aching need and drew him out of a protective, introverted shell. For a while, he was enraptured by the release and comfort of sensual passion. Her willing embrace defused his tensions, and allowed his tormented mind to be lulled and refreshed. In a sense, he was rescued from his own demons. I know he recognized the enormous debt of gratitude due her, albeit never fully expressed when he left, or should I say fled, the farm in such a hurry.

"Ack, there he is now. Look at that, he's driving a car! Good for him. I'm delighted that his journalistic career has prospered. Imagine the unpredictable, and then add the improbable, and what do you know, you come up with Daryl as his paper's unlikely expert on Jewish stuff. And by a half-breed Indian, no less. Surely it could only happen in America. Like Daryl said when he described himself, 'I might look like an Indian, but I have a love of literature and the arts which were inherited from my mother's Celtic genes.' But the price Daryl paid was steep: along with the creative talent came their weakness for alcohol. So . . . no one's perfect."

* * *

After their customary friendly greeting, they sat down on soft upholstered chairs in what had become their private corner of the lounge. Daryl's wet coat was draped over an adjacent wooden chair. The Rabbi nodded approvingly at his new raincoat with an attached hood, which served instead of a hat, an item Daryl curiously seemed to dislike.

"Vell, boitshick, so tell me, what's new in the journalistic world?" the Rabbi inquired. "But first, I must get in a complaint about your paper. They still pander to the public's voyeuristic appetite for violence and deviant sexual behavior. Nonetheless, if that pays for the meaningful news, buried though it is in the inner pages, even with skimpy in-depth coverage, then the cost is understandable. We must not forget that the ongoing fiscal viability of the paper does support your splendid articles. The recent one, about the comparison between the Jewish Lunar based calendar and the rest of the world's Solar based calendar, was certainly special. I bet most people never heard of the difference. Your article clearly explains why the Jewish holidays occur at different times each year. As a Jewish chauvinist, I admit our use of the Lunar calendar sets us apart, and incidentally also reinforces my perverse sense of celebration. You see, Daryl, despite all the age-old hostility towards my people, which might have pressured us to at least eliminate this area of friction, we have nevertheless tenaciously, which some might deem stubbornly, held onto our own calendar. It's a minor triumph of the particular, in a world that seems headed for a loss of distinctions, with prevailing pressure for more cultural assimilation.

"Please don't let me digress so much, Daryl. Back to your article. As a matter of fact, not only did I enjoy the piece, but I also learned some new stuff. Your impressive research added meaning and interest to the story. Vhoops! There I go again. Ask a question and before you can catch your breath, I'm off on a tangent. Zeit mir ("forgive me")."

Daryl smiled widely. He thought, how disappointed and troubled he would be if the Rabbi was taciturn instead of talkative. He knew when the Rabbi rambled on like that, he fired himself up and became flushed with youthful vigor. A remarkable display of his positive engagement with life. Daryl had become exceedingly fond of the Rabbi, and on some level viewed him as a father figure. Further, he readily acknowledged to himself how inspirational the Rabbi's life had been, and how he had benefited from the relationship in myriad ways. "Life certainly takes unanticipated turns, he mused." Abruptly an appalling intrusive thought caused him to shudder: *What if I had never met him? But, maybe it's my turn for good things to happen. After all I wondrously survived 'Nam without a scratch, and also miraculously met the Rabbi at a critical moment in my life. Best not to think too much, nor ask too many questions. All I know is how eagerly I always look forward to these visits. Something almost magical enfolds each time we get together, for which I am ever grateful."*

Yet, in the back of Daryl's mind a niggling anxiety kindled: he dreaded the inevitable day when he would be greeted at the Home with the devastating news that the Rabbi had died. He didn't need to be reminded about death. After all, having witnessed too many young men's lives cruelly snuffed-out in Vietnam, its awful finality had been irretrievably embedded in his consciousness. But with the Rabbi it was somehow different. Daryl felt Nam was a distant world, unreal and dream-like in so many ways, where he had been emotionally shutdown and hauntingly out of it.

Daryl worried that when the day came for the Rabbi to die, he might crack, and seek comfort in alcohol again. These upsetting thoughts—the Rabbi's death and his own potential breakdown back into alcoholism—terrified him. So, when he once again found the Rabbi alert and cheerful, his joy was reinforced with a deep sense of personal relief.

"Izak, I trust all is well with you?" asked Daryl trying to sound cheerful. "No more kranheit ("sickness")?" he asked with a broad smile—pleased with his use of Yiddish.

"Couldn't be better," brightly replied the Rabbi. "I feel all charged up. Sitting here in the comfort of the lounge, warmed by a cheerful wood fire blazing away in that massive fieldstone fireplace, and with a good chaver ("friend") for company—machen zaier naches ("makes for much joy"). And, so what should we talk about today?"

"I was wondering about your Easter holiday," said Daryl. "Oh yes, I know you don't celebrate Easter, yet something special in your tradition approximately coincides each year. I should know, but frankly I can't remember. I'm probably confused, with all the Jewish stuff I've learned."

"No problem, Daryl. I know what you mean. Didn't I warn you that all this Jew stuff is like a labyrinth with innumerable byways? Well, you've learned a lot, and I bet you know more about us than many a young American Jew knows about his own. So, it's Passover you want to hear about," answered the Rabbi, nodding enthusiastically. "O.K. Here goes. And do I have a super-duper story for you."

* * *

The Imberlach Imbroglio:

"As you would expect, the Passover story is complicated. Jews like complicated ideas. They relish digging into all the possible meanings of even the simplest and most direct statement. Some Jews even entirely devote themselves to unraveling the myriad trivia within our sacred literature. Maybe better they should work on a good tennis serve, eh?

"Now, Passover actually represents one of Judaism's most brilliant creative traditions. Brilliant is a big word, but it understates its impact. First, some perspective would help explain what I mean. In Christianity, for instance, going to church every week is important. Priests and Ministers usually don't hesitate to reproach parishioners they hadn't seen in church. Attending regular church services are meaningful obligations of faithful Christians, with noncompliance considered consequential. Jews, on the other hand, are also supposed to pray regularly, and attend Synagogue, but most Jews don't. It's a curious paradox for the nonobservant Jew: While practice of their religion was downgraded, still at the same time self-identity as a Jew survived. What is happening, I suspect, is that many Jews consciously (as vell as subliminally) think of themselves as members of a people—or even a nation—which undergirds their Jewishness. They also don't believe it inconsistent as Jews to be apathetic towards active religious participation, or even hold agnostic and atheistic views. Some express skepticism, too, about the relevance of all religions. This sense of people-hood is unique to Judaism, distinguishes it from other religions, and likely confuses some non-Jews. As a result, many Jews connect to the Jewish people without any specific commitment to the group's religion. This attitude—or maybe I'll call it a personal view— doubtlessly is free-flowing and open-ended, but does provide for the inclusion of a widely diverse membership.

"On the other hand, the Orthodox Jewish communities hold their own members to strict adherence to specific dogma, and often don't hesitate to voice their disdain for nonobservant Jews. Such open antagonism likely alienates some Jews. Certainly an unnecessary self-destructive tension is provoked among the Jewish people. Maybe it's even a form of masochism. When you consider there are so few Jews in a world filled with billions of people, I can't help wonder what those Orthodox are thinking. We have enough trouble with hostility from others, so we don't need any from within our own.

"Oh, the Orthodox—a minority of American Jews—do spend a lot of time praying. Yet, in my opinion, the glue that holds the Jews together are the festivals that are celebrated in the home, not in the

Synagogue by the religious minority. Here's the genius. The informal family home is where all can assemble: adults and children; believers; agnostics; the whole range of Jews; as well as non-Jews. Simply stated, the feast is open to any wishing to attend. Furthermore, no declarations of fundamental beliefs are a precondition to participation.

"Passover stands out as preeminent among all Jewish festivals. Let me tell you, Passover has become so important that we even have a special book, the Haggadah ("Hebrew meaning telling") to guide the feast. In addition to 'telling' the story of the historic Exodus, the sequence for eating the meal itself is cleverly woven within the text. It's veritably like high theater—an eclectic mix of spiritual, historical, educational, infused with lessons in virtue, and all combined with a heady balance of the mundane. Although these incomparable Haggadah texts have been open to infinite editing and adornment through the years, nevertheless, they all adhere to the same basic Exodus tale. It's unsurprising that Haggadahs collectively are the most published Jewish books in America. The Haggadah presents the Exodus in a memorable dramatic style. It chronicles our people's redemption from slavery to freedom—the powerful, quintessentially formative event in Jewish history (a worthy object lesson to those seekers of freedom around the world). The struggle for freedom of body and spirit is difficult, for which a steep price is paid, but the rewards are immeasurable. The message of the Exodus is as relevant today as it was when it occurred . . . over three thousand years ago. The telling of this provocative story through the ages as an integral part of family feasts, has kept it alive, as well as strengthening the self-identification of many Jews.

"The special name for the Passover feast is Seder ("Hebrew meaning order"). Central to the Seder are the wonderful foods with unique dishes linked symbolically to the story. It's hard to say whether the menu's attraction alone, or the Seder's stirring account of the Hebrew's Exodus from slavery in ancient Egypt, followed by the remarkable unfolding of the genesis of Judaism, has drawn people to this celebration. For most Jews—it's estimated that eighty percent of Jews gather for Seder—the combination is irresistible.

"Among all the various tasty dishes at a Seder, the inclusion of matzah is essential. It's hard to imagine Passover without matzah—a very thin, unleavened (no oil of any kind, simply flour and water) cracker-like bread. As you would expect, it has little ta'am ("flavor") of its own, but lends itself to an infinite variety of matzah-containing recipes. The 'alleged' origin of matzah connects to the rushed flight of the Hebrews from Egypt (Exodus) when they didn't have time to bake bread. Thus, they simply mixed flour mit water and created a flat, unleavened bread (maybe an apocryphal myth, but an appropriately imaginative one). Matzah has become known as the symbol of Jewish salvation, also called the bread of affliction, and while it might be considered a poor man's bread, it serves symbolically as a reminder that humbleness is a virtue. Keep in mind, that the Jewish redactors of our oral traditions never missed a chance to weave into the tale a message of ethical rectitude.

"Now we come to the heart of the tale. You must first forgive an old Rabbi his lengthy speech, in sermon-like fashion, instead of coming directly to the point. Alas, a professional weakness."

Daryl smiled broadly, waved the Rabbi to continue and said, "It's a wonderfully rich story, which I have been trying to capture in my notes. Izak, please go on."

Daryl's encouragement brought a smile and nod from the Rabbi, who then resumed.

"I'm not going to bore you with all the various foods, and how they cleverly embellish the Exodus story. Matzah is where I'll focus. Since Passover is fundamentally observed as a joyous occasion, honey and nuts—appealing foods enjoyed way back in Biblical times—are widely incorporated in many dishes. Which brings me to the particular sweet treat called Imberlach. It's a cooked honey and matzah confection, with a generous addition of ginger ("imber is Yiddish for ginger, thus Imberlach loosely translates to little gingers"). Sounds straight forward, where you would imagine there was a standard recipe. But, that's not the case. Jewish cooks like to be creative, so the recipes for Imberlach vary. Usually the recipes were passed down from grandmothers and mothers, but their differing national origins created variables. The Jews absorbed some culinary ideas from the gentiles, had to make substitutions due to the unavailability of traditional ingredients, and the recipes changed.

"Thus the evolution of divergent Imberlach.

"Here's just a few samples of Imberlach recipes:

1. honey, farfel (small broken pieces of matzah), filbert nuts, ginger, vater.
2. carrots, sugar, ginger, almonds.
3. matzah flour, ginger, eggs, honey, sugar.
4. honey, sugar (vhite and brown), farfel, ginger, valnuts.

"So, what do you think? Every balebosteh ("housewife") defended her recipe as if it were the eleventh commandment. After a while, people forgot how some distant relative changed the recipe in a moment of 'imagined inspiration.' From then on it became gospel. Who would know that the new concoction didn't taste as good as the original? That's the way traditions are made. For a while the recipe is passed along by mouth, until one day it is written down. From then on it becomes as carved in stone."

The Rabbi paused, and with a wry look, added in a rather solemn tone, "You know, Daryl, one can't help but view the sacred books of all religions, as having gone through a similar evolution, and are thus vulnerable to the same weaknesses. They all started long ago in the same way: some people, invariably old men, told stories.

"The good story-tellers were admired and quested. After all, what do you do on a cold rainy night in a cave, without television no less, but hope to gather around— with luck they'd discovered how to make fire by then—and hear a story. As time went on the stories were embellished with messages and signals supposedly gleaned from the all-powerful God(s), which stirred wonder and fear. Before long, the gifted story-tellers were elevated in the eyes of the people as possessors of magical gifts, and consequently they acquired an inordinate influence over the life of the group. Thus from simple story-teller there came into existence a novel, highly venerated person, with extraordinary power. This phenomenal development was greeted joyously by the people, for they now felt more secure than ever before. Naturally, a special name had to be assigned to those wondrous, and indispensable wise men. They became known by many hallowed titles: Shamans, priests, priest-doctors, witch-doctors, medicine-men, witchs, healers, and magicians, were some common honorifics. Although they weren't the secular leader of the group (tribe, nation) their influence over the chief was considerable. Chiefs were easily replaced following their death, or if they didn't effectively serve the needs of the group. Shamans, on the other hand, had unusual gifts, with unfathomable powers. When a new Shaman was needed, the group suffered extreme anxiety and an unsettled sense of crisis ,until a suitable replacement was found."

"It's interesting to note," interjected Daryl, "that modern clergy, as the heirs of the Shamans, still exercise considerable power. They hold sway over the lives of vast numbers of people, and are still expected to consecrate the coronation of Monarchs (although infrequent in current times). Moreover, it is not unusual to find instances of clerical efforts to influence political affairs and decisions. Curious how the power of the mystical still survives down to the present day."

"Ah, yes, Daryl. You're right. Along with the acknowledged infinite progress of civilization, humans are basically the same as they were back in the dawn of history. There's a disconnect between man's inventive genius and his basic nature. With all the religions run by these same humans, we shouldn't be surprised that some are capable of self-serving corruption and evil. But, despite this failure to

live up to their own dictates, we are confronted with a difficult world in which the
only guiding voice for peace and harmony
among people, comes from these same
religions. Flawed and abused, religion still
is the only sane voice in the wilderness."

Epilogue

No one was sure of the Rabbi's age, including his son, Paul. Somehow the subject never came up. But Paul knew his father looked older than he was. The emotional and physical trials of his life had taken a considerable toll. Paul understood from his medical studies how the cumulative impact of stress could drain a person's energy reserves, adversely impact the immune system, increase vulnerability to disease, and lead to a shortened life expectancy. There was also no doubt that Izak Asher had partially offset the negative experiences in his life with a positive, forward-looking attitude.

Nonetheless, the sad day came when Izak's life came to an end. Paul was notified by the authorities at the Home, that when his father hadn't appeared for breakfast—his notoriously favorite meal of the day—a nurse was sent to his room. She found him in bed, on his back, with the blankets neatly in place up to his chin. His blue eyes were wide open, and a smile lit his face, as though he were pleased that his time had come. All indications were that he had died peacefully during the night.

Paul had anticipated this day with much anxiety, and was grateful that his father had lived as long as he did. His emotions were deeply felt and highly complex. Paul's sorrow for his father's death was genuine and profound, while at the same time he breathed more freely now that the burden of daily concern for his father had ended. The stark irretrievable finality of life's end is unsettling and traumatic, although its universal inevitability is anticipated. So, Paul's unrestrained despair at his father's death shook him abysmally, and alarmed his wife at his surprising behavior.

Paul's inability to forget his father's unspeakably terrible years in Europe deepened his grief. Instead of rejoicing at his father's successful new life in America, he tended to somewhat downgrade or overlook it—he focused narrowly on the negative past. Izak sensed his son's burden and tried to dissuade his response by never offering to talk about the painful past. He hoped that his avoidance of the subject signaled its diminished relevance, and his intention to move on with hope for the future. Yet, Paul had put together through the years, from assorted glimpses, an understanding of much of the death-camp details. Although he personally wasn't a survivor of the Holocaust, Paul identified psychically as if he had been. He was gripped with the conflicting emotions of shameful guilt for his safety here in America, along with thankful relief that but for the grace of God he had been spared that horror. Paul was unable to shake these obsessive thoughts, although cognitively he recognized how overblown and unreasonable they were. Nonetheless, they had become permanent intrusions— like the PTDS (post traumatic distress syndrome) recollections that plagued Daryl.

Additionally, his deeply felt distress over his father's past suffering was perversely linked with his own unfocused bitter anger. At times he was overcome with a frightening rage, which was ultimately self-directed, as no suitable outlet could be envisioned. He suppressed these feelings as best he could, but they lurked closely under the surface, and effectively discolored his view of the world. No one, including his wife, realized their depth, and that he continuously struggled with these troubling passions. People viewed him as engaging, friendly, certainly bright enough, but a bit too serious, and attributed his personality to his profession as a dentist. Paul's conscious efforts to hide his true feelings, and specifically his contentious instincts, were outwardly successful, but their denial caused much internal stress. His father's death awakened a barrage of unsettling powerful feelings, which Paul had difficulty dealing with.

Furthermore, despite Izak's insistence that Paul shouldn't worry about him, or take time away from his busy dental practice and young children and wife, Paul ignored his father and had conscientiously looked after him. He had no regrets on that score.

* * *

According to Jewish tradition, the funeral was held promptly. Few people were in attendance since Izak Asher's relatives had all been lost during the Holocaust. Paul with his wife and two children were all that remained of his family. Their friends came, as well Paul's wife's relatives who lived in the city, along with a few of Izak's acquaintances from the Home showed up . . . and of course, Daryl was there.

Paul had met Daryl, in passing, at the Home on a few occasions, and understood how much his father had enjoyed their conversations. When Daryl showed up at the funeral service in the Synagogue, Paul, on the spur of the moment, asked him to say a few words.

Daryl was taken aback by the request, but after Paul explained that it was customary for people close to the deceased to address the mourners, he agreed.

While listening to the memorial service Daryl thought to himself that the prayers intoned by the officiating Rabbi and joined in by a few of the congregation were likely to be in Hebrew not Yiddish. Though unsure about the distinction, he based his impression on having heard Izak pronounce both languages.

To Daryl, Yiddish sounded a little 'sing-songish,' while Hebrew in contrast was guttural. For certain, he decided, this was not a Reformed Synagogue. Yet, neither did it seem quite like the very Orthodox service he had attended. "Well," he said to himself, "as Izak once explained, 'Don't be surprised at the wide diversity of Jewish worship practices.'"

Concerned about what he would say when called on, he remembered the rough draft of an article he had written celebrating the life of the Rabbi that by chance was in his jacket pocket. He took it out and scanned the text for ideas. Very quickly he concluded it wasn't helping, only making him more nervous. He decided he would try to be brief and speak from his heart.

When Paul signaled Daryl that it was his turn to speak, Daryl momentarily hesitated. But, when he looked at the Rabbi's coffin, placed in the front of the sanctuary, Daryl imagined the Rabbi looking at him with his warm encouraging smile and nodding head and Daryl knew he couldn't disappoint him.

"Shalom alaichem. I'm Daryl Wincoat, the goy who writes the Jewish column in the Herald." He paused, smiled broadly, looked around and added, "If you're surprised to learn that, you can't imagine how surprised I was when it came about. Actually, it's all Rabbi Asher's fault. He took one look at me, not too many months ago, and saw one broken young man, trying to pass himself off as a journalist, and reached out to befriend him. He became more than my friend—he was also my mentor, and by far the best teacher I ever had. It didn't take me long to realize that chance had put in my path a rare and exceptional man. Izak, and he insisted I address him as such, was my confidant, whose own story of survival during the German Holocaust helped me put into better perspective my troubling memories of the harrowing experiences I had as an army grunt in Vietnam. For that alone, my debt to him was immense.

"Significantly, I don't believe I ever knew a Jew before I met Izak, let alone knew anything about their religion. That all soon changed. Izak didn't hesitate to candidly answer my questions—including his own critique of Judaism embellished with learned comments—while simultaneously he exposed me to his rich Yiddish culture. That old language is amazingly expressive, and I admit to have adopted a few of its words.

"I must entirely credit Izak with how our dialogues developed. For the most part, he answered my many questions about Judaism indirectly, by telling stories, each of which revealed a segment or aspect of Jewish life. I learned that Judaism was like a fabulous mosaic—each segment a gem in its own right, yet held together by powerful bonds.

"Then, most remarkably, he urged me to base my newspaper articles on the essence of his stories. When I protested that I felt guilty about using his material, he said that the world now belonged to my generation, and furthermore, the public would better accept stories about Jews when told by a gentile. He was right; people liked my articles and asked for more.

"But our relationship was not one-sided. At his urging, I also told stories. At first I was reluctant to talk about my family, but Izak didn't let that pass. With his help, I opened up and soon began to better appreciate my own heritage. Incidentally, I'm a real mix: equal parts Apache and Irish. Additionally, when I questioned the relevance of the past, I'll never forget what he said, 'If not for the people who came before us, we would not exist. Therefore, the question is not who are we . . . but who were they.'"

"Rabbi Asher's wise counsel helped me change: instead of dwelling on the negative past, I learned to accept it, and moved on; the present became the time to set the stage for the future, which one can effectively mold and each new day as it opens is the future. So don't waste the opportunity, but relish the time afforded, and do something meaningful. Izak also made clear to me that over-and-above the tendency to focus on one's own needs, there are infinite needs outside one's self, to which you should offer help. Central to Izak's view of the role, or should I say responsibility, of man, is expressed in that marvelous Yiddish word, rackhmones ("compassion"), which for him was the governing principle. At times I got the impression he believed Judaism's most significant contribution was its emphasis on compassion.

"Certainly, Izak was also a pragmatist and realist, which understandably his life's experiences had taught him. He could express himself in incredibly insightful ways and redact complex issues into poetic-like simplicity. I will try to render an example as best I can—when he wondered, 'Is there something about the human spirit that defeats satisfaction and prevents contentment, unsettled as it often is by a strange yearning for the intangible and inexpressible?'

"Oh! . . . How much I'll miss him."

Paul was overwhelmed by Daryl's words. He suddenly realized how little he really knew of his father. Literally speechless with emotion, Paul approached Daryl, reached out and grasped him by his shoulders, and with tear-filled eyes, pulled him into a tight embrace. Both men broke into sobs. Their mutual embrace was prolonged, and cemented a lasting bond.

About our Author

Howard S. Selden is the author of over thirty scientific papers published in Dentistry's Journal of Endodontics (root canal therapy). During his career as a practicing Dental specialist he was also involved in teaching: he is a former Clinical Assistant Professor, Department of Endodontology, Temple University School of Dentistry, Philadelphia, PA; he helped establish Dental Departments in local hospitals to care for the indigent; and served as the Director of the Dental Department at the Muhlenberg Hospital Center, Bethlehem, PA.

Following retirement, when asked, "What are you doing with yourself these days?" he answers that looking back on his life, wondering what influenced him and how he got here, led to the fulfilling solitary experience of writing stories.

Having spent many years reading publications of all genre, it is not surprising his first published book, *The Pariah Stigma,* flowed easily.

The Shaman and the Jew, a historical fiction novel, is a complex creative effort. Selden found the blending of fictitious characters and plot within an authentic historical framework a continuous challenge. His long-term interest in history helped. The many collected books, especially those on ancient history, offered handy reference for pertinent details. Access to supplementary information through a computer search was invaluable. From Selden's earliest days as a Boy Scout, where he earned Eagle Scout rank, he recognized his interest in helping the injured and sick, leading inevitably to a career in Dentistry. In high school his role as manager of the football team offered many opportunities to aid the injured players, since in those days the helmets were soft leather, and there were no face or mouth guards—thus dentists were kept busy replacing displaced and broken front teeth.

As a long time alpine ski enthusiast, Selden, along with his wife and three children, enjoyed many a winter vacation on the winter slopes. At present, Howard lives in Easton,

Pennsylvania with his lovely wife, Tamara. There he spends many hours doing intensive research in preparation for his next work.

Selden's books are available from his publisher, A-Argus Better Book Publishers, website: www.a-argusbooks.com. The books can also be found or ordered in the better book stores or online from amazon.com or barnesandnoble.com.